ITNA

@ugman

a novel

Mark Sarvas

ITNA PRESS
Los Angeles, CA
www.itnapress.com

Mark Sarvas. -- 1st ed.
ISBN 979-8-9882829-8-3

Library of Congress Control Number: 2025937291

For Jennifer

"I can't keep away from it. I can't forget it. It haunts me day and night. It's the only thing in all the world that I am fit for, or that's fit for me. Oh, the dreadful river!"

—Charles Dickens, *David Copperfield*

"I have become solitary, or, as they say, unsociable and misanthropic, because the most savage solitude seems to me preferable to the society of the wicked, which feeds only on betrayal and hatred."

—Jean Jacques Rousseau, *Reveries of the Solitary Walker*

June–December 2019

Part One

MY UNDERGROUND DREAMS

@ugman

I am a sick man... a spiteful man. I think
my brain is diseased.

3:19 AM · Jun 1, 2019

Panopticon

I am a sick man... I am a spiteful man. I think my brain is diseased. (I nearly said *soul* but I don't believe in those.) I am unattractive. I am an abscess, infected, my heart filled with pus. I am prone to screaming rages. So much screaming. It was not always like this. Yes, I have run hot all my life. Perhaps the kindling was always there. But this, this is something new and terrible. My rage is a phantom limb, it follows me everywhere. It itches constantly, and I cannot scratch it enough. I have no beliefs. I have no appetites. I delight in my farts, which rumble like approaching thunderstorms. I joylessly masturbate every night out of momentum, habit, compulsion. I subsist as a vessel for my hatreds. I wake up furious. I go to bed furious. I move through my days in somnolent wrath like some murderous sleepwalker. I stare into the blue light doomscrolling until sleep overtakes my jittery, cortisol-flooded body. These are my words, these are me, I have worked through them all, they have had their way with me: bristle, explosion, outburst, uproar, convulsion, agitation, vehemence, frenzy, paroxysm, spasm, fit, eruption, raving, choler, spleen, ire, bitterness, acrimony, indignation, umbrage, squall, apoplexy, conniption, mania, rave, rant, boil, fulminate, seethe, shout, gnash, warpath, rampage, berserk, blustering, cyclonic, frenzied, fulminating, infuriated, livid, maniacal, dudgeon. Furibundal. (Obsolete, like me.) Fuck. Fuck fuck fuck fuck fuck all of you and all of me and all of it everywhere.

Try tweeting *that* shit, people.

280 characters, my ass. Enough with these fits and starts of rage, these hourly pinpricks of adrenaline, these snotty little bon mots. Twitter is a prison movie. You enter an innocent, unprepared for the steady stream of violence. Gradually, you become swept up in the invective, the fury, perhaps even instigating some trouble of your own. To survive, you tell yourself. To blend in.

Because nothing matters any more anyway. Because no one is looking. Because everyone is looking. You live on your guard, ready to respond to every perceived threat or slight. And by the time you are paroled after weeks, months, years, your eyes are dead. The wrongfully accused hero returns to the world deformed, deranged. Broken. Only the hatred remains. Or no, not a prison movie. A gladiator flick. Last one alive in the ring, stumbling punch drunk and bloodied but standing. Or a rom-com, only you're the ugly friend no one wants. Or a post-apocalyptic sci-fi epic. Or an action thing, all noise and frenetic cuts. Or a Christopher Nolan joint, mock profundity masking incoherence and hollowness. Ginsberg: I saw the best minds of my generation destroyed by madness. Twitter: Hold my beer.

What the fuck was I saying?

4:17 AM · Jun 1, 2019

TWMD

I keep lists of obituaries I am eager to read. These used to be mental lists, recited under my breath in the middle of the night to help me sleep, my personal choleric mantra. But the list grew too long to remember, and I began to write down the names. First on scraps, whatever was at hand: napkins, chocolate wrappers, used tissues, all jammed into my pockets until I could return home and transfer them to a fresh roll of butcher paper hung on the wall, under the heading "Those Who Must Die." Nothing on my phone. I felt the urge to *write* these. In ink. On paper. Permanence. Once I jotted a name on my palm, the smudged "M… ch McCo… ll" barely surviving my hand wringing long enough for me to make it back and add it to the scroll. Sometimes I would be unable read my own scrawl, the gouging, jagged lines indecipherable to me, though the impulse that animated them remained, and I would wonder: *What can I have been thinking?* In my suicidal moments, and there are many, I pull myself back from the brink by resolving to outlive them all, to cackle over their obituaries, to squat and empty my bowels on their graves, if I can find them. I envision a viral social media series of images, *#FecesontheDead*. My final, triumphant gesture, revenge for all the rage they have implanted in me.

Room

Except for the occasional nocturnal sally, I don't go out, not anymore. Not since they left me. Everything is delivered to me now. Left on my doorstep. Food. Laundry. Medicines. I survive on a small inheritance from a distant relative, my great-aunt Bettina who promised to remember me in her will if I could recite "Ode on a Grecian Urn" for her by my tenth birthday. The lines stay with me to this day:

> *And, little town, thy streets for evermore*
> *Will silent be; and not a soul to tell*
> *Why thou art desolate, can e' er return.*

I eat a single meal each day. My overhead is low, the rent on this room half the payment I used to make for the Audi I abandoned months ago in front of the nearest Walmart. Keys inside. I have no idea what became of it, and I don't care. Perhaps it still idles in that oceanic parking lot. I have nowhere to go, and too much to hate right in front of me. I pay for everything with cash which I keep in my mattress even though I abhor cliché. My twelve-foot square basement chamber is a far cry from the comforts of my old life, but it meets my meager needs. The wallpaper is torn and smudged with the meals or blood or tears of previous tenants. The wood floors are buckled, uneven, prone to throwing up splinters. It's always cold, always damp. The sounds of the city filter in all night, sirens, shouts, breaking glass and clattering steel. A single, street-level clerestory window looks onto the bare brick facade of the sardine cannery next door, long abandoned, though I swear I can still smell the rotting fish. I have a bed, a cot, really, that wouldn't be out of place in a military barracks. A card table and a folding chair. A plastic desk lamp. I keep one change of clothes in my narrow closet, though I spend most of my days naked, at my desk, with my computer. I steal Wi-Fi from the deli off the lobby.

...

My only other possession of any value is my guitar. A 1965 Höfner 500/1 bass. You'd recognize it in an instant, it's the same model as the violin-shaped bass Paul McCartney played with the Beatles, albeit right-handed. It lies under my bed in a state of perpetual rebuke, a pulsating reminder of my failures, yet I can't seem to part with it. I've shed everything else along the rutted path to this dank room but the Höfner clings to me like a terrified child. I used to pull it out from time to time; its sunburst symmetry and white binding still managed to give me a jolt of pleasure, until I realized I didn't want that pleasure, any pleasure anymore, that it was holding me back from my calling, my purpose, this repertoire of *ressentiment*. So, I banished it and that whole catalog of joyful music that, for a time, allowed me to believe I was part of something grand and wonderful.

Avatar

My handle is @ugman. Get it? My homage to Underground Man, my avatar, in the original sense of that word. Honestly, I can't get through the book—how fucking boring can you be, did no one tell Fyodor about this thing called *plot?* —but I do love my fellow basement dweller's splenetic asides. Of course, most of the mouthbreathers out there won't get the reference, and at first I worried about some smartass calling me "ugh-man" or responding "ug" to my posts, that sort of predictably banal Twitter repartee, but I have only eleven followers and I'm pretty sure they are all bots.

I follow 5,833 accounts. This imbalance of followers to followeds once infuriated me but over time it liberated me. Bots won't report my foulness, after all. I now take a perverse pride in the lack of reaction and interaction with my posts. It's such an echo chamber of logrolling and ass-kissing that I've come to see there's something noble in my solitary, neglected feed, like Churchill in the late '30s, disgraced, exiled from power, yet railing against the Nazis. Smarter than everyone around him. My finest hour.

No, I'm fine with this lack of attention. It frees me to utter every thought, every coarse impulse, no matter how vile or violent. Pure id. I can rage rage rage to my heart's content, no need to wait on the dying of the light when I can hasten it right now, right here from my keyboard. Some days, I can't type fast enough. The venom spills out of me, unchecked, at times incoherent and nearly illiterate, my brain charging ahead faster than my fingers.

Plus autocorrect. I once rebelled against its fussy, puritan tyrannies, but now it is my oracle, my digital Delphi, and I do not change its interference. I leave its corrections to speak for me. Here are some things that autocorrect has taught me:

I am internal with my baggie.

To give two ducks is generous.

I have a twitch that cannot be scratched.

Furibundal furibundal furibundal you cockpit.

Them

What was it like before, a life free of this hatred? My memories are dissolving shadows. I had a wife. I had a daughter. They are gone now. Left me, I think, though perhaps I left them. Events are cloaked in a white haze in my memory, like those last rungs of Jacob's ladder. My wife was a decent woman, full of compassion, and I drove her away with my feeling of triumph every time I edged her toward cynicism. Breaking her down became my project. Convincing her the world was shit. She resisted for a long time. But I was relentless. Am. I would celebrate every victory, every triumphant sliver of gloom and despair I pressed her to concede. And then she was gone. I wasn't surprised, not even a little. She was merely confirming my grand unification theory of the world, of its shitiness and the shitiness of everyone in it. (Autocorrect wants desperately to change *shitiness* to *shininess* but on this one I stand firm, you Panglossian tyrant.)

My young daughter went wherever it is her mother went. She screeched at me "I HATE YOU," and at one time it would have unmoored me, knocked me over and out. Instead, the words "Right back at ya, you little shit" rose unprompted in my throat. I might have tried to stop them or I might not have. I only remember her clawing rage, white and unhinged and directed at me, and it was as though I was looking in a mirror.

Sometimes I imagine she is one my eleven followers.

Avatar (2)

The kid has her own YouTube channel. She is twelve. Will the humiliations never cease? She has three thousand subscribers. *Three thousand.* For what? Watching her play video games and talk about them? Her most popular video has nearly twenty thousand views. I am an ouroboros of pride and diminishment.

There is something mesmerizing about her. She has a presence, there's no doubt. She is smart, authoritative, and witty, even though I only understand every third sentence or so. This is a side of her I never saw, this confident, competent avatar. She was a cheerful toddler then an angry teen and then I was gone. I scrutinize every word, looking for some coded message, hoping against hope she might actually mention me some day. It's become a ritual, I return each Saturday for her latest drop. She's reliable enough though sometimes she does fall behind schedule and I am inconsolable for days.

Sometimes I interact in the chat with her, but this, too, fills me with unbearable sadness. Anodyne exchanges, abbreviations I mimic from her other followers.

Jan-Gaming 393: Spooky!
StayShrimpy: Yay!
Hayleyxoxo: Dang so good!
Mr. PP: why is there so much bots here christ
UGMan: Awesome!

She is dutiful, reads through every single comment, clicks a like on each one, including mine. It isn't much, this impersonal brushing by in the crowd, but I'll take it.

Numbers

I used to observe the Sabbath. It seemed important. Not sure why. Some slim connection to what was. Same as with the music, the Höfner. I hung in there long as I could, but the last few attempts were sheer agony. The blue button calling me. That's some real addict shit, I know. Not only did The Twitters make me miserable, but forsaking what was left of the parts of me that mattered? That was even worse. Double trouble. Still, even after they left me, I tried. One small window, a protected pocket. Offline. Just me, myself, and I. Alone with my thoughts. With God. The two of us, *mano-a-mano* in my little room. I imagined these protracted dialogues, Him trying to straighten me out, scare me of out my stupor; me stubbornly clinging to…

G: *This won't do, you know. This won't do at all.*
Me: *(silence)*
G: *Don't sulk. Does no good. I know what you're thinking. Be not quick to anger.*
Me: *(silence)*
G: *I don't actually have a mother, you know.*

For reference: "Be not quick to anger, for anger lodges in the bosom of fools."
So says Ecclesiastes (7,9)
This is, of course, horse shit.
God told Moses to *talk* to the rock. And he *struck* the mutherfucker instead. Got his water just the same.

That last Sabbath, I tried. Slid the computer under the bed, next to the Höfner. Got dressed. Lit a candle. Mumbled the prayers. I paced. Stared out the window at the feet clomping past my eyeline. Made my bed and remade it. Opened a book and stretched out. I lasted twenty-six minutes. Each one felt like my intestines were being tugged out through my esophagus an inch at a time. I gave up, booted up, fell down. I've had orgasms that didn't feel as bad/good. Little death, indeed.

Senator (1)

Those Who Must Die: Entry 315

This senator, I fucking hate him.

It started out as simple political differences. Garden variety left/right bullshit. The stuff of progressive dinner table imprecations. But it got worse, perhaps because he kept prevailing. Because his only end seemed to be power in and of itself. This simple hatred grew in time into something more. He undoes me, this senator. He preys on my dreams. With every act, he ignites me, underscores my impotence. Each morning I log in and I find the latest reminder of his soulless core. I can't envision what keeps him alive, what propels him through each day like some robotic, hungry shark. He surely has no internal organs, no viscera, no hot blood in his veins. I take the fact of his continued existence to be a personal affront. He lives to spite me, I'm sure of it. There's no blue pill for this kind of impotence. Just a blue button.

There's a thrill that attends every one of these missives. I get a little dizzy and short of breath each time I click the Tweet button. That I can ruminate so openly about his death, even wish for it, and go unnoticed, unreported. The old taboos swept aside. Good manners are such old hat. And so the sentiment is out there in the world. Perhaps one day he will see it. Perhaps someone will retweet it and I will go viral, hundreds if not thousands of likes. The expression of a desire that I know sits in the breasts of those too weak and fearful to give it voice.

Online I am a warrior. Heroic, a leader. A man of action. Alone in this room, nothing can silence me.

Yet to encounter me on the street is to mark me as a coward. Meek. Eyes downcast. The kind of guy who sometimes shoots rock stars and presidents but mostly writes manifestoes and nurses every slight. I have written 50,000-word blog posts (remember those?) full of swagger and venom and impeccable reasoning, but they signify nothing. It's just me, this room, and the eleven of you. And so, I wish the senator a lingering and painful death with a clean conscience even as I know that he will continue to swim through black waters with dead eyes and razor teeth.

Swing

I'm sixteen. Muggy suburban Sunday. Cicadas whirring in the trees. Tall grass in the park jitters in the wind. Leon and I are walking together, practicing a harmony I can't seem to get right, making our own little nowhere plans, when we notice a neighbor of mine standing in the middle of the park with a golf club practicing his swing. For some reason, we find this pantomime of middle-aged athleticism hilarious. We laugh, catcall, say stupid shit like, *Where's your ball, man?* It's unclear how long he is aware of our sniggering, whether he is ignoring us or simply can't hear. But, at last, he stalks over to us, club in hand, menacing, furious. He wears sandals and loose fitting polyester shorts.

I strike an unaffected pose but am relieved for the fence between us.

You little shits, he snarls. Hitler should have finished your whole family.

He stomps in the direction of home. Leon and I are shocked by the venom of this, briefly abashed. And then Leon breaks into uproarious laughter. I join him, not feeling it, but wanting our departing Nazi to hear it: You can't touch me.

Walking back to my house, Leon wonders: How did he know? Could he see our dicks?

Here's what she didn't understand, my kind and compassionate wife. She had this quaint notion that we should speak to or understand our enemies. The very word *enemies* discomfited her. What is their pain, she wondered. Meet them in the middle. Compromise. Unity. Understanding. Well-meaning platitudes.

I knew better. We must destroy them. Before they destroy us.

Though it's already too late.

So I keep here in my room, aware that I'm part of a time-honored tradition of Jews hiding out in tiny spaces. Doing my bit. I track their hatred, their movements. I follow the marching pinpricks of tiki lamps like dots on an air traffic map, wondering how long it will be until they try to come from me. I'm ready to fight them, want to fight them. Want to snatch my neighbor's club from him and smash his skull until greypinkwhite jelly oozes from his ears.

seethe (v.)

*Old English seoþan "to boil," also figuratively, "be troubled in mind, brood" (class II strong verb; past tense seaþ, past participle soden), from Proto-Germanic *seuthan (source also of Old Norse sjóða, Old Frisian siatha, Dutch zieden, Old High German siodan, German sieden "to seethe"), from PIE root *seut- "to seethe, boil."*

—Online Etymology Dictionary

A small herd of elephants has settled into the room next door. This is most unwelcome. It disturbs my subterranean isolation. They are five: a man, a woman, and their three vermin offspring. Obese, noisy, Southern. Mississippi twang fills the night air as they bellow at each other. The things they are to me, the things I am not allowed to call them: White trash, trailer trash, ghetto. They thump against my walls until late into the night, intruding on my thoughts, derailing my grand plans. I pounded back once, my tiny, impotent fist barely disturbing the thin wall that separates us. For a moment, their hubbub paused. I heard laughter, and then answering thumps rained on the wall and the chaos resumed. So I lie in bed awake until the wee hours, devising ways to murder them in their sleep and get away with it. This, I tell myself, is the brake on my violence, this last part. I have no wish to martyr myself, after all. Without my freedom, I can't continue my fight. This is the lie I tell myself, that I would if only I could get away with it all.

My heart is racing, and I taste metal in my mouth. Sleep. I can't sleep. I must sleep. Fuck the Senator. Fuck the elephants. Fuck them all.

The Good Fight

This is what my shrink told me, once, I think.

Anger originates in the amygdala. It identifies threats and starts sending out fight or flight messages. (Thank god for the genius of Twitter, which lets you fight and flee at once.) I'm told this part of the brain comes online before the cortex, which is the seat of reason and judgment. So much online discourse is explained by this fluke of body chemistry—the brain is literally hardwired to goad us into action before we fully understand the consequences of those actions.

(You can only cancel me once, mutherfuckers.)

Our muscles get tense, and our systems are flooded with catecholamines, which give us that Incredible Hulk-like burst of energy that sends us lifting cars or subtweeting. The heart rate climbs, blood pressure soars, breathing accelerates, and there's one message above all the others: *do it, now; do it, now*. This is what I feel all the time, my pissed off heart banging against the walls of my chest, demanding my attention, which has become so narrowed and focused that I can only see the 280-charactered object of my hatred. Adrenaline primes you into a state of arousal, ready to tear, to kill, to shred, to tweet. This is the worst part, the way the adrenaline can linger for hours or even days. The physical rage stays in the body long after action is taken. The heart keeps racing after the thoughts have moved on, pulling you back, reminding you of your rage. Sometimes I tremble and wobble for days. Other times, I wake up in the middle of the night and, as soon as consciousness materializes, I try to flee from thought, desperate to prevent the endless perseveration and the flood of adrenaline that keeps me awake, ill, battered. It never works. The thoughts always find me. My eyes are still open as the sun nudges through the blinds, and I lie there in a blind haze. Lost and confused.

Where did the hours go? I honestly don't remember. My shrink also explained that this over-arousal works against memory, against recall. The more ramped up, the harder it is for new memories to take root. Is this why I seem to be missing so much about my wife? My child? Yesterday? Or is it better this way? Like returning to childbirth, this river of forgetting ensures that I can continue, doing my work, fighting the good fight.

My shrink fired me, by the way. Badge of distinction.

—I think we have come to the end of our course together.
—You're firing me?
—No. It's not that kind of relationship. But it's clear that we have not made the therapeutic gains either of us might have hoped for.
—So you're firing me?
—I can refer you to a few people who might be a better fit. Here are a few names.
—Furibundal.
—I'm sorry?
—Just thinking about a tweet.

Seven Days

I have a system, I run a tight ship. I like things nice and orderly as I ascend my weekly Everest of apoplexy. I'm a creature of routine, as uncool as I know that is. It goes like this:

I maintain seven lists, each one comprised of hundreds or thousands of accounts I follow. These lists are alive like coral, expanding and shrinking and reforming as the furies do their worst. I'm constantly adding, removing, enhancing, overlapping. (Take the cancer-riddled radio "personality" who ended up on three lists before he finally had the decency to drop dead and spare us another moment of his hateful existence. I still keep him in the lists, go back to gloat over his demise. Very satisfying.) I immerse myself in one list a day, though some days it does give over to randomized chaos. Generally, though, we start the week out with a bang, Monday is all about "Right-Wing Assholes." Tuesday, I hop over to "Racist Shitweasels and Conspiracy Freaks." Wednesday, I cozy up with "Flaccid Mainstream Media Shills." Thursday, I spend with "NeoCon Mediocrities." Friday is set aside for "Woker Than Thou." And Saturday culminates with "Brooklyn Literati." Sunday is for "Puppy Memes." Nominally a day of reset, though if you think those can't piss you off, you aren't doing it right. I tried to keep a list called "Good News." It never contained more than a dozen accounts. The very concept felt foreign to me. It withered, unattended. So puppies it is, my one sort-of concession.

Meditation

My wife suggested I meditate. Stay in my body. Feel the physicality of my rage to work through it, without being distracted by my *narrative*. My *storyline*.

Her words. My life as tall tale.

I tried. Downloaded a popular meditation app. Followed along with "WillyBee," some silky voiced guru coming at me "from the calm center of existence." I started small. Two minutes. Two hours. Two years. Two lives.

Breathe in, hold it, and release. Feel your body.
Fuck
If your mind wanders, don't judge.
Piece of shit.
Notice it. Maybe label it - "thinking."
Fucking asshole.
Return to the breath. Feel what's in your body.
My hummingbird heart. (The hummingbird's heart beats at 1,260 bpm, for the record)
Think of something or someone you feel grateful for.
Um…
Exhale your stress, your tension. Breathe in a clean new day.
Bluebuttonbluebuttonbluebuttonbluebuttonbluebutton…

Hummingbirds go into a state of torpor at night so they don't starve to death. Neat trick, that. I miss torpor.

Hammer

A brief story of my father. He told this one often. He was a young man, probably in his late twenties. He'd saved his pennies and bought his dream car, a used Austin Healy Sprite. Candy apple red, as he recounted it. I looked up the car years later, an absurd smiling thing, bug eyes and a puffy cheeked grin. One afternoon, he found himself behind an old beater that had failed to move when the traffic light turned green. After what I am sure must have been an indecently brief interval (my extrapolation, absent from his telling), he began to lean on the horn. And I do mean *lean*. I'd seen him pull this sort of move when I was a kid. The beater refused to budge and my dad refused to relent. After who knows how long, the beater revved hard, threw into reverse, and crashed into my dad's little sports car, wiping the grin off its face. With a little forward thrust, the beater untangled itself from the ruined grillwork of the Healy. Before they got too far, though, my father snatched up a hammer that had been sitting shotgun, and he hurled it at the retreating beater, shattering its back window as it sped away. I think often about the absurd pride he took in that gesture. Did he think he'd bested them? Got his own back? The hammer is the obvious punchline of the thing, the foul, impulsive grace note. But what I think back to, what I fear most, is that first, long intemperate beep. The impulse to be as loud a dick as possible. Every night, the thought crosses my mind: am I just leaning on my Twitter horn? Has this been in my blood from the start? (Nurture, nature, Twitter?)

Office

Your angry musings do not align with our corporate image.

I had a job, rather a good one. I didn't detest it; it paid very well. My clients liked me, I mostly liked them. Kept us all in reasonable comfort and security. An office with plants and a coffee machine of my own. An assistant named Max. American fucking dream, yo.

We have received customer complaints.

Back then, I posted under my own name. Foolishly. I had a whopping seventy-three followers but I used hashtags, trying to ride the popular waves to get noticed. Got noticed right out of a job.

Did you, in fact, wish for the death of politicians? (The printouts directly in front of them.)

I was briefly a *cause de celebre* of people I loathed who decried my "cancellation," a "casualty of woke." Right-wing hacks. Libertarian goons. Quills in hand, these reactionaries rode to my rescue. What sad, limp bullshit. I was canceled by capital. No one is "canceled" because business interests have come to Jesus. Profit is the only morality that moves the needle. I was still explaining all this as I was escorted out of the office. Max looked away, refused to meet my defiant eye.

DM

Setting aside the political and philosophical implications, the rabbit said as he slid into my DMs, *perhaps it's not such a hot idea to wish people dead?*
     This, I knew, was his way of asking me *what has become of you?*

(I do love that joke: A priest, a minister, and a rabbit walk into a bar, and the rabbit says, "I think I might be a typo." I've always loved that bit of rabbity hesitation—it's the polite and uncertain "I might" that sells the joke.)

He offered me a ticket to Yom Kippur service, my rabbit. He was just trying to help me, I know he was. I'd lost my job, he could see what was coming next. I told him I thought ticketed services was taking the whole "chosen" thing a bit too literally. I said other things, showered him in my disdain, wanting to see if I could get him to block me. He held fast, replied with verses:

"Though the mountains be shaken and the hills be removed, yet my unfailing love for you will not be shaken nor my covenant of peace be removed," says the Lord, who has compassion on you.

Remember not the sins of my youth, nor my transgressions:
According to thy lovingkindness remember thou me,
For thy goodness' sake, O Jehovah.

Why boastest thou thyself in mischief, O mighty man?
The lovingkindness of God endureth continually.

In the end, I blocked him. His unflappability unnerved me. And I thought, maybe the typo is me. My crap runneth over.

Trigger Warning

I think about buying guns all the time. I peruse the online advertisements, lose myself in the minutiae: action type, trigger type, grip finish. I stroll through the aisles of gun shows, hands thrust deep in my pockets, casting sideways glances at the wares on the tables. I imagine the bulk, the heft in my hand. I've never actually handled one; my cowardice is too great. I fear those moments of despair, when a convenient gun might offer me too-quick release. Sometimes I fantasize about marching up to these enemies of mine, leveling the gun at their chest, and pumping three bullets into them. It's always a tight three, for some reason. Definitive. I imagine the report, sometimes I quietly make a popping sound, a forced exhale through tightened lips. Other times I imagine the gun placed under my jaw—the submental triangle it's called—and release a single round I never hear. I feel soiled by these daydreams, cheapened and coarsened by my violent, animal nature. Consumed by the paradox that I would never dare act on them. Perhaps you consider this latter a triumph of civility, of norms. Perhaps it is. But from where I sit, it's one more break in my tattered psyche, all tweet and no action. I read these news reports, reports of the men who snap (it's always men) and act out with deadly finality. They sicken me. I hate these base brutes, these inarticulate, enraged cowards. And then I fall back onto the slenderest of threads that separates us. Who blows on that thread? How much can it bear?

No, no guns for me. I abhor violence, really I do. I will rage, I will vent. But I'm a peaceful man. I leave the dirty work to others.

Glock me, Amadeus

Outtakes

When I told them I'd been *terminated*, there was pity from my wife (she called it "compassion" but, like cilantro, there was no hiding its foul flavor), and scorn from my daughter. I think. In these odd little gaps where memory should live, I keep running the outtakes. The director's cut of my life.

Take one: In this version of my memory, I stammer out the words "I've been let go" whereupon they both begin to laugh and point at me and mock me with expressions like "turd-boy" and "schmuck-face" and "limp biscuit." My wife wipes tears of laughter from her eyes, her mascara running like some kind of murderous goth clown, while my daughter slaps a perfectly formed thumb-forefinger L to her forehead and runs around me in excited circles. I wet myself.

Take two: In this version of my memory, I pull myself straight and, with a devil-may-care shrug, advise them that, "They fired my ass today," whereupon they both go a bit pale, sink down onto the couch and immediately begin strategizing between themselves as to how they will get along and make ends meet with only an occasional shameful glance my way to remind me that I have any role in this narrative whatsoever. I wet myself.

Take three: In this version of my memory, I decide to hold off telling them altogether. It will all come terribly clear soon enough. As with every director's cut, we'd all be better off with fewer extras.

Undertaker

I'm ten, visiting my grandparents for the summer in their apartment in Vienna.

I can still summon the smell of their apartment building. The ground floor housed a leather goods shop, and the entryway always smelled of handbags and shoes. The elevator had a metal grate that you had to pull closed before you could operate it. The floor of the lift was on springs and required the weight of an adult to press down on it before the door locked and the buttons were activated. It moved slowly up the six levels, scraping the sides as it rose. A staircase wrapped around the elevator shaft, and I could always outrun it to the top while watching my grandparents rise through the frosted glass.

One afternoon, I decided it would be a hilarious prank for me to hide in the shadows with my beloved plastic cap gun and leap out all 007-like as my grandfather exited the elevator. He was a kindhearted and cheerful man despite having summered at the Mauthausen concentration camp and my idea of fun was to scare the crap out him. What could go wrong?

I waited around his usual homecoming time and before long I heard the telltale scrape of the elevator. Through the frosted glass, I could discern a solitary, elderly figure. I crouched on the stair, just around the corner and above the elevator door, ready to pounce out the moment the door opened and shout "BANG!" Which is precisely what I did.

A crack from a gloved hand on the side of my head, and my cap gun went skittering across the landing. I didn't cry. Normally I would have, but I was shocked into silence by the sharp, brute violence of the thing.

It was not my grandfather. This man was taller, older than my grandfather. Dressed in a black suit, he looked like an angry undertaker. And angry he was. He shouted at me in German, though he sounded muffled and far away in my ringing ear.

He pointed at the three doors, a pantomime of inquiry. Where was I staying, this was his obvious intent. I feigned ignorance, shrugged. *English*, I kept feebly insisting. Affecting as stupid a face as I could muster. He raged again, pointing at the doors, clutching me by my shirt. I was terrified that my grandmother would hear the commotion and investigate, but the doors and walls of the old building were thick and sturdy. At last, he released me with a disgusted sigh and stomped up the final flight of stairs to his door. I stood on the landing, silent as a tree, until I heard the confirming lock of his door. I scooped up my pistol and retreated shaking into my grandparents' apartment, closing their door as silently as possible, and ran to the guest room, where I hid out for the rest of the day, terrified that the undertaker would show up making inquiries that evening.

He never did. And I began to grow angry. My father hit me all the time, but for this stranger to clean my clock so thoroughly for what was obviously a childish prank. How *dare* he? I stewed all night long, unable to sleep, concocting elaborate revenges. On the day I left my grandparents, I shat into a small bag and left it in front of the undertaker's door.

Some nights I look at their apartment via online maps and street views. The leather goods store is gone but the building is otherwise unchanged. I tilt up so I can see the sixth story, estimate their unit, the room where I cowered, hiding from the undertaker. My grandparents are long gone, and the undertaker has no doubt met his own. So why do I keep going back, looking night after night?

Because it's there. Because I can. Duh.

Here Comes the Sun

Disaster. The deli cut me off.

This morning their guest Wi-Fi connection was locked. Password required. I could feel an immediate tightening in my chest. The panic rising. The stream continuing without me. With every minute, I was missing—what? Everything. Now I was truly insignificant. My voice silenced. Alone.

Anything but silence. Can't bear that.

I dressed myself. First time in weeks. How strange the press of clothes feels against my skin. I made my way up to the lobby via the stairs, avoiding the elevator and other people. Blinking like a groundhog in the light of day. I hurried into the deli, ordered a Monte Cristo sandwich and asked for the guest password. The sound of my own voice foreign to me. I talk to myself at times in my room, usually when I am working out a longer, more complex idea. But this kind of interaction sounded false, like an actor in a play. I waited for the sandwich, eyes downcast, desperate not to make any kind of unnecessary contact, not to see or be seen, and hurried out of the deli as soon as it was ready.

I can't recall the last time I was outside. Weeks. Maybe months by now. I paused for a moment between doorways and, in spite of myself (or to spite myself), I turned my face up to the sun. Eyes closed. I stood there for a moment, natural warmth on my face. I took a deep breath, smelled the cool tang of the river. There was a brief tug, the pull of the natural world, held so carefully in abeyance for so long, asserting itself. Before I could feel anything more, a voice I recognized as my own whispered to me:

Me: *This is not for you.*
(Crazy long pause.)
G: *(Stage whisper) Only I can make a tree.*

Slap

Something unprecedented has happened:

A like. A solitary handclap. (Autocorrect would have it a lie, but I feel its electrifying veracity.) I am of two minds. On the one hand, there's a sliver of satisfaction. I was proud of this one, the marriage of high and low, a coarse death wish with a Canterbury pedigree. Why shouldn't it be noted, lauded even? Yet it undoes my hot streak, my empty, loveless existence. I can't even claim perfection in neglect, in insignificance. And if someone is truly watching, what will that bring? Do I have to watch myself now, temper my wrath? If I don't, will the authorities come knocking at some point—or worse, might I lose my account? You laugh, but to be cut off in this way would be asphyxiating. To be removed from the slipstream of now, the current of hatreds that animate me, keeps me moving like Frankenstein's creature. Why couldn't the world have just left me alone to rant?

Still, it's a good line, isn't it? And who is this mystery liker? Not one of my loyal eleven bots. No, it's someone called @NevskySoldier. He follows no one, no one follows him. Like me, he travels light. Not a trace of him to be found. No other likes—just me. A discerning fellow. But this is the problem—now I am aware of him. Do I perform for him? Tailor my thoughts to garner his approval? Perhaps he didn't intend to like it; perhaps it was an errant slip of the thumb, like the brushing of shoulders on a crowded street, barely registered. Or perhaps it's a slap, a rebuke, a challenge. An "I'm watching you, mutherfucker."

Jab

It's time for some kind of action against the elephants, who haunt my dreams. Shortly after 3 a.m., I creep into the corridor. I unscrew their hall light, placing the warm bulb in my pocket. I drizzle maple syrup on their doorknob. And I take away their tattered doormat, though given the threadbare condition of it, this may be more favor than vandalism. I've considered graver penalties, thought about ways to set fire to their rooms, but can't come up with a way to do this that doesn't threaten my own space. So I content myself with these jabs, blows struck for my honor. Put another way:

@ugman

Suck it, elephants.

3:07 AM · Sep 22, 2019

Survey

How pleased with your rage are you?

It exceeds all my expectations—extremely satisfied.
It meets all my expectations—satisfied.
It falls slightly short of my expectations—somewhat satisfied.

Other:
<u>*It is, like everything else, a galloping fucking disappointment; predictable, overwrought, pointless.</u>

And so we beat on, boats against the current, borne back ceaselessly, flailingly, snarlingly into our impotent fury.

English majors are the ducking worst, amirite?

Chains

Something they don't tell you, that vast Corporation of They, but maintaining your righteous anger is exhausting. I mean physically. Most days by mid-afternoon, I can't keep my eyes open. I drift off, short naps, spittle, snorts, cricks and I wake even more tired. The cycle unbroken, perpetual, eternal fatigue. Too angry to sleep at night, scrolling, reading, linking, viewing, hopping, until I pass out, phone in hand, stirring with first light, drained, sick to my stomach, heart tired, I mean pumping slowly effortfully reluctantly—*tired*, like a *why are you making me do this* kind of tired, and I never wake, not really, not fully, always a weight I'm dragging around like Marley's chains, a scrim of fatigue that never lifts no matter how much espresso I down, and even then I dread the night when I know sleep still won't come because there aren't enough distractions in the world to keep my heart from doing this unbroken tarantella of despair and fury, and my brain is against me, telling me stories, fucking *narratives* all through the night and I just want to kill someone, something, even me, just to make it all stop.

(Click here to unsubscribe.)

Games

Sometimes I play computer games with my daughter. Her game handle is easy to remember: mydadissuchanasshole. I've created dozens of temporary IDs just so I can follow her around these virtual worlds, watch from afar as she picks up scrolls, disarms bots, levels up. She plays with an intensity and focus that is so familiar to me, but she's more cautious than I am. Not a risk taker. She contents herself with modest, consistent gains.

Occasionally I try to interact with her—all in disguise, of course—but I taught her well about the dangers of online psychos and predators, and she ignores me.

Unsent letter one.
Dear little bunny,

Do you remember when we used to walk every day, and you would talk and talk and talk and tell me about your latest game, your new strategy, your frustration at being stuck on a level? You always apologized for going on and on, but I loved every moment. Such simple bliss, walking together, listening, riding the wave of your seemingly limitless enthusiasms. It filled in something in me, something empty and missing from my own desiccated, failing heart. I think about those walks often, and although I don't get out much anymore, occasionally, I wander along our old path, visit those haunts and for a moment I feel

No. Grief, it interferes with the rage, you see? Dulls its purpose. I have only one setting now. It's an eleven.

Unsent letter two.
Dear little bunny,

Watch out for the exit campers. You haven't figured out yet

that the best way to beat them is to draw them into the maze with the jeweled sword and then clean their fucking clocks.

Love,
assholedad

String Theory

Once a year, I restring the Höfner.

I don't know why I do this. I've broken all my other habits, as my hygiene attests. This one persists. I used to hate restringing my guitar, would pay a local luthier to do it for me. I didn't have the patience, the precision of mind and hand and heart to do it right. That tight, little, neatly clipped knot on the tuning peg was beyond me.

But lately I've been doing it myself. An excuse, maybe, to pull out the instrument. I don't play it, except for a quick riff once the strings are changed to ensure the bass is in tune. I work silently, efficiently, with a steadiness that surprises me. At times, I begin to slip into memories, recalling myself on stage with Barry, Rob, and Leon. The slightly musty smell of the velour-lined case sends me back to Rob's basement, to rehearsal. To the music. The fights. The betrayal.

Four strings

E, A, D, G

Barry, Rob, Leon. Me.

The E string fat like piano wire but flat and shiny like an eel. Never roundwounds, only flat. Mac Daddy would insist.

On the Capitol records release of "All My Loving," he makes a mistake on the bass in the second verse, playing F# and C# fifths against a C#minor chord. They let it stand. When we would perform the song, I would play the mistake. Fidelity and all that.

Lean on the horn. Play the mistake. Avoid the exit camper.

Senator (2)

The senator has died.

It's all over my feed today. There is celebration, mass exulta-tion. Much speaking ill of the dead, I note with approval. I am not, it seems, alone in my loathing. And I get, at long last, to scratch at least one name off my list of Those Who Must Die. That alone seems reason to rejoice. Cause of death mysterious, autopsy pending. He was old, broken down, leprotic both inside and out. I would like to think it some form of divine retribution, that even God himself had decided it was time to stop pumping breath into the bitter old bastard.

Building management has replaced the elephants' missing doormat with a new one. It's thick and brushy with a decidedly chemical smell. I glance at their tattered mat in the corner and realize that I have engineered their upgrade. Tonight I will swap out the doormats. I'm satisfied with this elegant gesture but dis-tracted from full enjoyment of my handiwork, as a darker idea takes shape. Is it possible, can it be, that perhaps the senator's death is the handiwork of my Nevsky soldier? A tribute of some kind to me? Did I plant the idea for this true man of action? An offering from an acolyte. Or a threat, some kind of warning? Sticks and stones may break my bones but tweets will really fuck up your shit.

You can post hoc fallacy me until my ears bleed, but I do not believe in coincidence.

I am uneasy.

And a little excited. Yeah, yeah, yeah.

I see you.

Part Two

APROPOS OF WHAT'S NOW

Key Indicators

When from dark error's subjugation
My words of passionate exhortation
Had wrenched thy fainting spirit free;
And writhing prone in thine affliction
Thou didst recall with malediction
The vice that had encompassed thee:
And when thy slumbering conscience, fretting
By recollection's torturing flame,
Thou didst reveal the hideous setting
Of thy life's current ere I came:
When suddenly I saw thee sicken,
And weeping, hide thine anguished face,
Revolted, maddened, horror-stricken,
At memories of foul disgrace.

—Nekrasov (translated by Juliet Soskice)

I recall an episode that won't leave me alone.

Once upon a time I was twenty-three and working at my first job, tie required, punch in, punch out. The regional office of a nationwide pizza chain. It was a job, I needed a salary, I took it. I didn't even like their pizza. "Death discs," I called them, though never to my loathsome supervisor's face. She was a humorless scold who tried her best with me, I suppose, training me in all the weekly reports I needed to prepare. Advising me about my appearance. Handing me a copy of *Dress for Success*. My contempt for her was total. I wanted to shake her and say, "it's just fucking pizza for chrissakes!" The office had a keypad lock on the front door. Every time a person got fired, she would change the code and distribute it to all of us.

Every Monday I had to punch in by seven a.m. and begin the work of transcribing what they called their "Key Indicators" — the number of pizzas sold at each store the prior week. I fielded calls from Hawaii, Arizona, Washington, Texas. Franchise owners shooting breathless numbers my way, each determined to outsell the other. Managers spoke with hushed reverence about the "keys," as they called them. It was an absurd culture. People seemed to live, die, breathe, dream and fuck pizza. I took none of it seriously, laughed at them as I produced reports full of mistakes. I wore wrinkled shirts and cheap, clip-on ties.

Dress for Success tip: Avoid garish patterns on ties that can distract an interviewer

The company was owned by a born again Christian. When the one Jewish VP was up for promotion to regional director, HQ sent out corporate investigators who interviewed me. A pair of them, clean cut, dressed like Mormon missionaries. A sinister interview. Darkened office, shades drawn. What did I know about his private life? Apparently there had been some chatter. Was he honorable? Appropriate around women? I refused to answer. Told them I had no way of knowing when what I wanted to tell them was to fuck themselves. I wanted to tear my tie off, throw it at their feet, and storm out never to return. Instead, I sank back into my desk, typed up the daily logs while browsing porn underneath. Pepperoni and pussy. Anchovies and anal.

The VP was not promoted, not with a name like Weinberg.

The Monday after my interview with the Mormons, I caught my supervisor in the process of reprogramming the front door keypad. She smiled when she saw me pass. "I'll hand out the new code at the morning huddle," she said. Her friendliness surprised me. She barely made eye contact with me an hour later as we sat in her office and she fired me. I fiddled with my Mickey Mouse necktie as she explained I wasn't Death Discs Material. She escorted me to my desk, watching over me as I boxed up my meager belongings (New York Mets pencil cup, Eiffel Tower paperweight).

"You don't have to hover," I said. "It's a fucking pizza company, not the Pentagon."

Later. I said that later. In my head. When I played back the tapes. In reality I was mute as she marched me out the door.

Dress for Success tip: Ensure that clothing is clean, pressed, and not too tight.

That night, lying in bed, I rehearsed my angry speech. I would return the next day and deliver it. Or call her. Or deliver a registered letter. That I would sue, wrongful termination. That the Christians had fired their token Jewboy. That I would own her, own her house, own the whole fucking company before it was all over. That I held a grudge and had nothing but time on my hands. I would dedicate my life to ruining hers. That the world would know the truth about these shady anti-Semite, pie-slinging cocksuckers.

Dress for Success tip: Nobody thinks suspenders are cool. I mean it. Nobody.

I never followed through. I had defeated her in my head and that was going to have to do. Still, she pops into my thoughts from time to time. When I replay this episode, it isn't the firing itself that stays with me. It's the lie. The way she looked me right in the eyes and, without hesitation, told me she'd give me the code later. I busted her, caught her *in flagrante* and, instead of being honorable, owning up, treating me with an iota of dignity, she lied flat out, denied me my humanity, the basic honor one person should afford another. I realize that's a bit heavy for, you know, pizzas. But a man's gotta have a code, amirite? All in the game, as Brother Omar reminds us.

I occasionally wonder what has become of her. A few halfhearted and fruitless online searches. Then I realize that she is unlikely to have given me a second thought since I was frog-marched out the door all those years ago. And I am furious all over again.

Dress for Success tip: When in doubt, nothing is easier than naked. It makes a statement.

Scraps

Once upon a time, there was a girlchild who grew like a flower in reverse. Open and blooming and full of color at first, then contracting, vanishing, retreating into a tight little bud of anger. Chicken and egg. Me then her? Her then me?

I came into her room once while she was drawing something. She was nine. She shoved it into a book with a guilty start. I asked her if she wanted to share it with me. Fuck no, she said. Or at least, she must have thought. She shook her head, apologized. No offense, dad. None taken, bunny. I looked at it that night, once she was asleep. A stylized self-portrait, girl with cat eyes, paws, tail. The scrawled caption: *Why so sad?* The single teardrop a cliché yet moving. The next day she knew, somehow, that I'd looked. Screeched at me and tore it shreds, throwing the scraps at my feet. I collected them and tried to tape them back together. I keep it in my Höfner case, a gummy mass of yellowed cellophane. Frankenstein's jigsaw puzzle.

Key Indicators (2)

Arizona

Cheese Pies	3,777
Meat Lovers Pies	6,210
Hawaiian Pies	352
Other Pies	1,535

New Mexico

Cheese Pies	2,111
Meat Lovers Pies	5,351
Hawaiian Pies	1,008
Other Pies	877

Hawaii

Cheese Pies	1,777
Meat Lovers Pies	3.788
Hawaiian Pies	5,362
Other Pies	12

(And let me just ask right here, 'cause I know you're thinking it, too: What is *up*, Hawaii? If you made me Dictator for a Day, I'd revoke their statehood for this pineapple and ham abomination. No fooling. This is some Crimes Against Humanity level shit.)

What about *my* Key Indicators? How to account for oneself? What are the meaningful markers? We must have them, right? Stands to reason.

Account balance, zero.
Credit rating, 500.
Resting heart rate, 122.
Family lost: One.

No, it's not numbers, it can't be something we count. Nothing so mundane, so palpable. But if not that, then what?

If/then. Been asking myself my whole life.

Apollo

This morning, a knock at my door. The first in all the weeks—months? years? —I've been down here.

At first, I was sure it was a mistake, an errant flick from a passerby or a prank by one of the baby elephants. But a moment later, there it came again, someone gently rapping, rapping at my chamber door. With considerable trepidation, I wrapped a blanket around myself and cracked open the door. How long it been since I had performed this quotidian task, opening my door to another human being? How awful it felt.

I was greeted by the desk manager. A foul, greasy hipster who introduced himself as Apollo. What a sad bastard, a far cry from his luminous namesake. Black hair slicked back, multiple ear piercings. An officious manner, as though he was the concierge at the fucking Ritz. I felt a new entry on the list of Those Who Must Die taking shape.

The elephants, he informed me, had complained.

My minor mischief had been reported and, with no evidence at all, they suspected me. Apollo was there to ascertain if there was any truth to it.

I summoned as much dudgeon as a basement dweller wrapped in a blanket can fairly claim. I advised him, with a hauteur that rivaled his own, that I had absolutely no idea what he was talking about, was not even aware there were residents next door, and as a reliable, paying customer insisted that I not be bothered with such trivialities again. There was a wounded look in his eyes that gave me brief pause as I shut the door in his face. I lingered, listening carefully to his breathing and shuffling in the hallway, as he debated whether to prolong our interview. After a moment, a grunt, and then footsteps as he shuffled off.

I sat down at my desk, triumphant yet shaken. I'm shaken still, as I write this, the cacophony next door continuing, shaking my walls. How can they have guessed so quickly? What will happen next? How does this escalate? My rage rumbles like a volcano ready to blow. How dare *they* report *me*? Any pleasure I felt at my little acts of revenge is totally undone now. It's always this way, you *do* something and think that's the end to it. And then someone goes and *does* something back. And before you know it, it's all-out war.

And this little bastard Apollo? He thinks that he's better than I am, though I recall his injured pride, and I suppose perhaps he is. He has a job, a purpose, a life beyond these shabby walls. A station. Is that what I detect in him? Rough dignity? Or judgment, elevation over me? We may both know it, but there's no need to rub my face in it, is there? No, I will own him. He's nothing, a servant, less than that. You're on the list now, buddy.

Four a.m. I press chewing gum into the lock of the elephants' door. Then into bed with my phone. *Thumbsthumbsthumbsthumbs.*

Apologia

Turns out Hawaii is not to blame. I have wronged them and I apologize. (I, at least, am big enough to admit when I wrong.) Things I've learned:

Hawaiian pizza appears to have originated in Canada, of all places (hence the inclusion of the repellent Canadian so-called bacon), although it might have started in Portland, Oregon, which I suppose one should have seen coming.

It is also, according to Lord God Wikipedia, the most popular pizza style in Australia. Something about the Commonwealth clearly undermines discernment.

Thirteen letters in Hawaiian pizza. Not quite the sign of the beast but no good luck charm either. If you tend to notice such things, which I do. I came home one evening to find them eating it, mother and child. Ordered directly from Death Discs to boot. They smiled up at me between bites of steaming cheese and pineapple and I saw scraps of human flesh dangling off their lips and I ran to the bathroom and hurled.

Practice

An unwelcome pop up today from WillyBee, my one-time meditation guru. He's offering a live online series of lectures on reducing stress and anxiety. I started to delete the app but something held me back, something in that silky voice of his that made me give him another look. Five minutes on his website, all the usual clichés. One-time hedge fund manager, made three fortunes but ate lunches at his desk—as though that's the worst spiritual crisis that can befall you, cold Mickey Dee's on the blotter while you surf Huffpo or Drudge or Pornhub. So, in classic guru fashion, he chucks it all and begins his *practice*—why is it always a fucking *practice*, as though he's promising up front that you'll never get it right, not really. I was all set to shut the browser, wipe the app, and craft a multi-tweet series on the nexus of spiritual charlatanism and capitalism but this one picture held me up. Dude sitting Lotus position on the beach, huge curly white beard and long curly white hear, a teacup Yorkie sitting on his lap. He looks like a gay Santa Claus.

He looks so fucking happy I could spit. Blissed out little cockmonkey.

It's easy to be happy when you have seven hedge fund buyout zeroes trailing you around. Still. There's something in that smile that looks distantly familiar. My wife would smile like that sometimes. Perhaps that's why she liked him, why she suggested I check him out. I don't think you can fake that shit. God knows, I've tried.

A seven day course on calming. Probably a rip off, waste of time and money. Getting in touch with your inner crybaby and all that sort of 1960s Haight Ashbury jizz. I'm sure it'll just piss me off, this low rent spiritual cretinism.

Where do I sign up?

Wolf

Silence from @NevskySoldier. But he's still there. I know it. I can feel his eyes on me. Feel the pressure of him in the air.

The senator remains dead.

Does this make me an accessory? Did I, just maybe, somehow summon forth this true man of action into being? Every reaction wanting its opposite reaction, that sort of thing. The vacuum of me needing to be filled in the world and by the world. My light/dark opposite.

Last night I dreamt of him in the form of a wolf. Gliding through snowy woods. Steam billowing from its snout. Dried blood on the fur around its mouth. Eyes that are the opposite of the senator's; darting, alive, attuned, brilliant in anticipation. Looking for more.

What have I released into the world?

Seven Days (2)

I'm confirmed for WillyBee's online workshop: *Seven Days to Rebirth and Sacred Inner Healing.* Don't you wanna just puke?

Charley

It's nine o'clock at night when I crack my door open to retrieve my meds from my welcome mat. The local druggist and I have an arrangement. He drops my Adderall refills on his way home for a generous gratuity. I know what you're thinking, but I don't abuse the stuff. I go pretty easy except when I'm working up one of my grand schemes that just won't wait. There are nights when I spill out my tweets by the dozens, and a little pill helps me along. One bottle lasts weeks.

It's usually a pretty stealthy maneuver, as I like to minimize my time in the meatscape. Don my blanket cloak, crack the door open, crouch down, sweep in the bag, shut the door. Tonight, however, the bag isn't on the mat. It's in the hands of one of the elephant offspring. He's examining the bottle when the door opens. A little hockey stick leans against the corridor wall. He looks up and into my eyes, which are presently at crouch level.

Hi, he says with an unbearable sweetness. He's about five, I guess. His face is dwarfed by a mane of tiny blond curls. He stares at me with innocent eyes and I already hate this fucking moppet. Don't touch my shit, don't make me feel. We stand there regarding each other in silence for a too-long moment. He hands me my bag.

I'm Charley.

I take the bag from him, get painfully to my feet. His eyes follow as I rise over him.

I live there. He points at his door.

I nod.

Want to see my new gun?

He holds up a small plastic pistol for my inspection. I know he's just a kid. It's not his fault I hate his parents. But I can already see what he is turning into, what he will become. Hockey sticks. Guns. I've seen his older brothers around, a pair of skate punks riding up and down the hallway. At night they practice jumps on the sidewalk outside his window. Clattering endlessly, without a thought for anyone else. I close the door in his face, both satisfied and miserable. No. I don't want to see your fucking gun. Go away. I press my ear to the door and remain there until I hear his footsteps pad away down the hall.

Doomscroll

It goes like this: (uh-one two three FAWR!)

Thumbsthumbsthumbsthumbs phone hot in my hands screen undulating past like spinning fruits in a seedy Vegas slot machine my lists first right-wingers then anti-Semites then climate change deniers then anti-vaxxers then a puppy meme or two to catch my breath before back to Nevsky have you posted have you liked no thumbsthumbsthumbs ride a hashtag #shittymondays #workfail #wereallgonnadie add some follows new faces to hate chest already tightening like bands across it compressing little room to move to beat look there's that mutherfuckin' bowtie asshole again hate him christ I fucking hate him why isn't he dead another look at Nevsky nothing to report palms slick with sweat thumbs cramping and aching hours of just spinning the wheel here comes double zero here comes salvation here comes the thing that will make all the suffering comprehensible here comes the thing that finally puts me on top there goes the thing that isn't what I thought it was and I'm not who I thought I was but no one gives a fuck not even me because look at this shitty world it just keeps filling my screen and there's always more of it this running river of shit like we are all Pompeii about to be buried in the lava flow of our shit our hatred our hopelessness and still I read because my enemies are all out there posting marching taking the world away from us and can you believe this asshole which asshole all of them and I don't know how to get any of it back but this is the only place I can think to look the fucking answer has to be here just give me one worth reading one that makes some kind of sense one that suggests that I'm not just throwing my thumbsthumbsthumbs away or maybe if I shout loud enough I might matter more and I've heard of Traumatic Brain Injury and I'm wondering if Internet Brain Injury is a thing and if it is I have it and if I have it I think it's pretty bad and where is Nevsky why is he making me wait there's more to do so much more every day every night it keeps coming #hashtagsgoingby and I need to know it I'm expected to be in it I can't not know what is happening even if it brings nothing but fury can't not get the references even as they enrage me the only way to be in it is to be in it in it in it.

Innit?

Five minutes down. All night to go.

Ménage à trois

Sometimes I lie awake into the night and try to summon a moment. That first moment it all began to slide away from me. A pointless excavation, maybe, but something to pass the time. Yet a moment does come to mind. In bed with the wife, a little afternoon delight, our favorite. Rolling around with that familiarity of experience yet not without enthusiasm. A recognized sexiness. After a while, you just know where things are meant to go.

A glow, a buzz, a wiggle on the nightstand and something has happened. Mid-thrust I am distracted by my phone. A message, a text, a note, a like. And all at once I'm out of myself, the slipstream disrupted, my erection collapsing like a politician's resolve. My thoughts turn to the problem of checking the phone without seeming like I want or need to check the phone but I *do* need it, I *must* know, and of course she notices because she's not, you know, an idiot. She isn't addled by this addiction. I imagine I am being subtle, but her reproving eyes are on me as I check it under the guise of "silencing it and putting it in the drawer," but no one is fooled here and even though we more or less pick up where we left off, a sinister new third has joined us. Afterward, she leans in the doorframe, pulling her robe tightly around herself and whispers with that infinite compassion of hers that she's worried, perhaps I have a problem.

Flint

The language of rage may evoke heat: *burning* rage, *fiery* rage, *white hot* rage. But that's not my experience, for me it's all icy, freezing like snow. The world out there may be heading toward a slow boil but this little room of mine is always cold, no matter what is happening outside my window. It's cold on dark and rainy days; it's cold on bright sunny days. Some days the mercury edges above eighty and still I shiver. There's not enough of me to warm the space. I'd be warmer if they were here. That is one of them there universally acknowledged truths. I feel their absence most on the days I am coldest. Or the other way around. It's not *missing*, not really, too sentimental, too needy. It's just recognition: I am colder without them. My tweet storms rage the hardest when I'm coldest. Personal best: 128 tweets in an hour. 120 of them simply said:

The other eight: mydadissuchasasshole

No cutting and pasting, that shit is for pussies. Lazy ass script kiddies and shortcutting punks who don't understand the virtues of hard work. Each one typed by hand, bespoke ranting, fresh cuts made to order. A sputtering stream of rage to displace the cold, each one a piece of flint struck against itself, against me, against all of you. Waiting for a flame that never comes. And you think perhaps I have a problem?

Suspicious Activity

So, this happened. Grab your popcorn.

Another goddamned knock at the door this afternoon. At first I thought it was Apollo back to apologize or badger me more but there was a crispness, a sense of purpose in this knock that was unfamiliar, a contrast to his slothful scrape. It alarmed me. At first I didn't respond. I sat at my computer, holding my breath. Waiting to see what might happen next. Another crisp knock. Then a voice:

FBI, sir. Please open up.

What the shit?

I sat rooted at my desk, terrified. Sweating like a rabbi in a Spam factory. Nevsky's evil fruit, come home to roost, and other mixed metaphors. Had my erstwhile sonofabitch comrade hung me out to dry for the senator's death?

We can hear you breathing in there. Please open the door now.

I threw on my blanket, cracked the door, and peered into the hallway. Two of them. Straight out of some crap movie. Cheap suits and aviators. Hair a bit longer than regulation. Donut fans by the look of them. Wallets, ID, the usual. They were following up on reports of "suspicious activity." That's what they called it. What was I getting up to in there, on the computer all the time? They were admirably vague, never mentioned the senator or Nevsky directly. Canny bastards. Trying to get me to slip up, incriminate myself. Finally, I had enough.

Where's your warrant?

They looked at one another, and I'd swear they were laughing at me. We're just talking sir, don't need a warrant for that.

Well you need one to talk to me. Good day.

I slammed the door, kicking myself. *Good day?* Who the fuck says "Good day"? What is the matter with me? I'm pretty sure I heard spectral laughter echoing as they retreated from my door. None of this makes much sense. I realize they can work all sorts of magic tracing IP addresses, but I use a VPN and I still can't quite connect the dots that lead them to my door. Unless Nevsky knows who I am. Either way, I expect they will be back. I have three theories:

(1) They are what they seem to be and I'm screwed.
Or.
(2) Apollo or the Elephants sent them after me, ratted me out, some act of petty revenge.
Or.
(3) I have entirely imagined their visit, a sleep-deprived mirage.

Profiles

About a month ago, I created a profile on a popular online dating site. Pure fiction, my idealized self, a character who is "me." I just wanted to see who might answer, if there was any idea of me that might hold any appeal. To hear, I suppose, from another human being, even briefly. There's a fine art to the bullshit of these things, the ideal balance of good taste and self-deprecation, though not too much because then you lack confidence. A little humor, the occasional topical reference, a soupçon of earnestness, then simmer uncovered for hours. (We'll keep the truth between us.)

My Self-Summary
Flawed but learning, at peace with the world and my foibles, curious and working hard every day for me, for you, for everyone. (Prophet without honor.)

What I'm Doing with My Life
Learning. Something new every day, whether I mean to or not. (Tearing the mutherfucker down.)

I'm Really Good At
Hiding my light under a bushel. (Elaborate revenge fantasies.)

The First Thing People Notice About Me
How closely I listen. (Why so angry?)

Favorite books, movies, shows, music, and food
I have always found these answers to be too performative, virtue signaling, hey look at my impeccable taste, my "curated" life. So I won't play. But I won't embarrass you with a Coldplay playlist, I promise… ("Favorite" is a word that makes me gag.)

The six things I could never do without

I can't imagine being that connected to any thing, *any material object, that I couldn't live without it. The things that sustain me are love, family, patience, compassion, tolerance, and wisdom.* (High-speed broadband. Fuck all the rest.)

I spend a lot of time thinking about

Global warming, obviously. I mean what else is there, right? Everything necessarily takes a backseat to this one (or it should). Which isn't to say I don't worry about sex trafficking and migrant child separations. I do. I also generally ponder how best to make my way through the world, not just without harming others but doing something to make it all a little bit better. (Insults revenge slights loss parking tickets Bond movies confirmation hearings anti-Semites insurance companies credit scores dead parents living parents absent parents Pete Nevsky my kid my ex senators bowties Apollo elephants guns hashtags headlines pizza fifth grade sixth grade junior high Leon Barry Rob undertakers exit campers Pete feces cheaters losers thieves chords licks harmonies goddamn blue mutherfuckin button from hell and on and on and on and on *thumbsthumbsthumbsthumbs* lather rinse repeat.)

On a typical Friday night I am

Walking down by the river, inhaling, grateful for the end of the week quiet. (Not lighting Shabbat candles, that's for fucking sure.)

The most private thing I'm willing to admit

I don't know what I'm doing here but I'm trying. (I don't know what I'm doing here but I'm trying.)

You should message me if

Don't.

I do get the occasional message, perhaps one a week. Sometimes I'm moved, this slender reed, this sputtering attempt at connection across the void. Sometimes I'm contemptuous, how low have you fallen that *this* profile speaks to you? I don't reply, ever. Groucho Marx, clubs, etc. Sometimes they write back, irritated. *You think you're too good for me? I bet half your shit isn't even true. You must be short and have a small dick.* No one, it seems, cares to be ignored.

@ugman
I see you.
10:11 AM · Sep 24, 2019

Wet Snow

(Variation on a theme by John Lennon.)

I saw her once, on the same dating site. Lovers and friends I still can recall. (Some have gone. None remain.) I couldn't blame her, not really. Moving on and all that. But it was a blow, I won't lie. The worst part was the photo she used, the bright line so clear where I had been cut out. Our San Juan summer. It was easy to see why she chose the picture - the combination of her deep tan and her sun brightened hair was irresistible, then and now. She excised me artfully, totally. I might have been nothing more than a rumor, a phantom, an unexpressed desire. The trip now lost to me. Memories lose their meaning. Not her fault, though, this elision, this strange smoking gun gap of missing tape. I was attentive once. I'm sure of it. *Present*, as that larcenous twat WillyBee likes to say. Yet little by little, I began to… absent myself. Withdraw. Small lapses, easy enough to fake at first. A nod of the head, a meaningful grunt, a reasonable facsimile of engagement. Then a strange thing happened. I just stopped listening altogether. Like Hemingway's bankruptcy, gradually then suddenly. To everyone. The effort, the focus being more than I could summon, forever not for better. Not laziness. Absence. I simply stopped being there. I was always elsewhere, off in my head, suited up in this battlespace, fulminating to the exclusion of all else. Only so much oxygen to go around. My wife and I would drive home from dinner with friends and, as she recounted her impressions of the evening, I found I had no idea what she was talking about. In the end, I suppose her leaving me was merely making concrete the absence that was already underway in my head. The first step toward my eventual erasure. And theirs, though I often stop and think about them.

Niagara

As she got older, the kid developed a habit of holding in her pee with camel-like intensity. She'd be too distracted, too focused on whatever it was she was doing behind her closed door and then it was as if all at once she remembered how badly she needed to go and the house would shake with the thunderous footfall of a stampeding giant and she'd slam the toilet seat down and this great splashing exploding Niagara fire hose of piss would fill my ears followed by the deepest sigh of relief imaginable. It seems keeping everything inside to bursting is a family trait. Apples, trees; you know the drill.

Noise

Seven Days to Rebirth and Sacred Inner Healing.
    Day One:

Our first session. A live Zoom class on Sunday morning. Two hours. Capped at twenty people. First a lecture, then a guided meditation, then questions. I have to say, this WillyBee is one slick mutherfucker. He has the whole online teaching thing dialed in pretty well. Dashboards, handouts, reading lists.

I log in using the handle **FyoDos** and keep my camera off. We are encouraged, as WillyBee explains in those silken tones of his, to participate in whatever mode brings us the most peace, the most comfort.

Until now, I have only seen photos of the guy, heard a few recordings. Now, watching him move, alive in his space, I observe that same irritating blissed out lightness of being that came through in his photographs, the same lightness I sometimes saw in my wife before I wore her down. I can see why she liked him, I can see why she recommended him to me, foolish an idea as it was.

I can see why she is here. Now. In this very session.

(Light Induced Zebra Accelerator)

She looks awful. Pale. Broken. She's come to get herself back. I should leap out right now, quit this thing. I feel like I'm intruding, watching her on the shitter or masturbating. I don't belong here. I stay. Because, as we all know, as she knows, I suck.

WillyBee's introductory talk is a rambling mess, but I have to admit, he's got *something*. I can't really put my finger on it and maybe it's simply the train wreck of his cheesy awfulness, but I can't take my eyes off him. He starts off by explaining the format particulars and all the resources available. He tells us about his own "journey," nothing I didn't know for free from his website. Then he starts asking us questions. Rhetorical, he says. No one has to answer. Everyone should feel safe and comfortable at all times. *Safe* and *comfortable*. Sweet Jesus. What brought you here, he asks. What do you want to get out of our time together? What do you value? What do you miss? His lecture continues for an hour, seems twice as long but I'm already tuned out. I can't take my eyes off of her. She watches with that familiar intensity of hers. She's so decent and true, I could just scream. There is a weariness in her eyes that wasn't there before, that I know is my doing. It makes me feel sick, this confrontation with my depraved handi-work.

My daughter flits by in the background and I throw up, barely getting it into the garbage can.

She's grown into herself. Though it's just a fleeting image, I can see she moves with a new limber ease. Unhunched. Unbundled. Unfurled. Her hair is cut short, dyed deep purple. She's become someone else, someone new, and I don't know her at all.

WillyBee leads us on our first meditation. Sit comfortably, up-right. Limbs loose, feet on the ground, arms relaxed. Relax your body. He walks us through, step by step. Unclench your jaw. Re-lax your face. *Relax your fucking face*—how the hell are you supposed to do that? The whole idea feels slightly deranged, yet I can't deny there's a tightness exactly where he said it would be, stretching tight across my cheeks to the back of my head but hell if I can find the magic button that releases it. I'm distracted al-ready, trying to understand this Tight Face Syndrome when I notice he has already moved down, he's in the solar plexus so I've missed, what, shoulders? Torso? Throat, maybe? Can you relax your throat? Now's the talking about genitals, that crazy ass dip-shit actually says the word—*genitals*. Relax your genitals. Lunatic raving though I imagine relaxing my sphincter and flooding my shorts with shit or whatever else it is that is impacted within me, my *stuffing*. He continues on through the legs, down to each toe individually. It takes ages and by the end I'm more stressed and clenched than when he began. I keep looking to her, wondering how she is doing, looking maybe for guidance, direction but more likely just some sign that I haven't wrecked her beyond repair. She never opens her eyes, seems to be following along, relaxing. I can almost discern a weight briefly lifting as WB tells us to attend to our breathing. Breathe in to relax the mind, breathe out to relax the body. In for a count of four. Hold for a count of two. Release for a count of four. That's a lot of goddamn counting, but I guess the idea is if you're counting you aren't thinking about the rest of the tumultuous pile of shit that you call your life so maybe I can count along with him for a bit but mostly I keep cracking one eye open and peering back at her. After thirty minutes of this, I'm sweating, panting, worn out as though I've just run a sprint.

Once or twice in the session, ol' WB calls on me. Asks me a question. Wants to engage me. There are too many reasons not to answer. She'll hear my voice. They'll all hear my stupidity, my spiritual paucity. I use the chat to tell him I am on a month-long silent retreat. It's an impulsive reaction, borne of desperation, but it's a flash of genius. He begins to wax positively rhapsodically about the value of silence. I think the fat old bastard pretty well cums in his kaftan, and suddenly I'm granted this exalted status, unearned but I will take it. Other participants start messaging me notes of encouragement and support. She even sends me a message: *Amazing! Go for it!* I reply with a namaste prayer emoji, and she smiles a smile I haven't seen in years.

The Q&A is, as you can imagine, the worst. The vulnerability of it all, the earnestness just makes me want to puke. These middle-class strivers and their trivial problems all couched in self-help pseudo mantras. I listen to their banalities, and I'm struck by the sameness of their concerns, their narrow bands of worry. Sure global warming is a drag but the barista on the corner always spells her name wrong and she doesn't feel *seen*. Or he can't divine his purpose because his parents, who are still paying his bills, insist on *negating* him and he blah blah blah blah blah. Infuriating. I can't help myself. I ask a question just to fuck with them. Some ersatz profundity for the master:

FyoDos: Is the <u>noise</u> all there is?

A long silence ensues. Mostly, I mean them, their nattering, their self-involved moaning, and also him, the noise of his directions, of his prompts, of his so-called insights. But there's this other noise, the one that plagues me when they're gone, and perhaps WB means that one when he lands his blow:

WillyBee: Why do you think you hear it only as noise?

Bowtie

Nevsky has ghosted my ass. This meekness is unbecoming. I thought were *simpatico*, you and me. I thought you were for real. Are you just another disappointment, another poseur? It seems I shall have to work harder to flush you out. FBI or no FBI, it's time for the nuclear option. A quick review of the TWMD list leads me to a detestable bow-tied commentator. His program is a reliable conduit of bigotry and venom and still he rants on with impunity. Just the sight of his smug, ignorant face sets my heart thudding.

Let's put his head on the block.

Hang that racist punk from the rafters by that little bowtie of his.

12:00 PM · Sep 30, 2019

See? I, too, can be a man of action. Your move, Nevsky.

Homework

We have *homework* between sessions. Actual fucking *homework*. What an evil genius this asshole is, getting me to pay him to work for him. Homework has always infuriated me. I remember trying to help the kid with her fourth grade math homework, fractions and ratios and whatnot, shit I had long ago left by the side of the road. I got angrier and angrier with her impatience, with her "Dad you're doing it wrong that's not what the teacher showed us," as if the *how* mattered at all. Results, baby. My wife finally pulled me away as I started shouting and cursing at the stupidity of the public education system. My sheer indignation at having to go through the eternal recurrence of all this shit *again* was more than I could bear. And now he wants me to do *more homework*? It's not fractions, granted. It's not paperwork or labor intensive. He wants us to *think*. To *reflect*. To *assess*. As though this isn't what I already do, all day long. I thought he was going to help me *stop* doing all that. And he wants me to meditate. Every day. Is this the whole of his life? What the everloving fuck does he have to be so happy about?

Clap (2)

@ugman

Hang that racist punk from the rafters by that little bowtie of his.

12:00 PM · Sep 30, 2019

1 Like

I thought I'd lost you, buddy.

Now what? I'm exhilarated and terrified and exhausted and queasy and semi-erect all at once. Don't really know whether to laugh, cry, puke, or rub one out. Mustn't get ahead of oneself, of course. A Nevsky like does not a death bring, at least, not yet. Once around isn't dispositive. Still, it's hard not to imagine all I might do with this newfound power.

Of course, I don't yet know the cost of all this. Nevsky may come knocking to collect his due and then what? What is my responsibility in this Faustian bargain? I mean, looking around, he'd see I don't have much to offer by way of recompense. And anyway, if you plan to collect a fee, you better agree to terms beforehand.

No, I think we may be more of a Butch/Sundance kind of arrangement, I'm the brains, he's the muscle. Maybe he's been waiting to have his talents put to good use, to find someone he can trust to direct his mayhem. If so, this could be the beginning of a beautiful friendship. For now, though, it's just a like. And the knock on the door may still come.

Sides

G: *(sotto voce) Pssst. Remember me?*
Me: *(long pause) I thought you'd left.*
G: *I'll never leave you.*
Me: *Everyone leaves. Even you.*
G: *Would you like to know how this ends?*
Me: *Go away. I have work to do.*
G: *Furibundal.*

As God Made Us

Apollo is back in the game. Caught him in the act of sliding something under my door this morning. Flung the door open on the slippery bastard mid-crouch. He reddened, straightened, fidgeted. I opened the envelope. A bill. Replacement lock for the elephants' door. A printout of a grainy cell phone picture of me stuffing it with gum.

I threw the bill and photo at him. It's a fake, I won't pay.

He stood there, eyes downcast. Shuffling from foot to foot. Insisted I had to pay or there would be "consequences." Can you believe he actually said that? *Consequences?* Look at where I live, you little shit. What kind of possible *consequences* can you inflict on me, you rancid little cunt.

Again that wounded pride. Forlorn sigh. Eyes still downcast.

Look me in the eye, forfuckssake.

Then put something on, forfuckssake.

Dress for Success tip: When in doubt, nothing is easier than naked. It makes a statement.

I drew a blanket around my waist to spare his delicate sensibilities. We are all God's creatures, Apollo, all made in His image. Nothing I have that you don't have, you big baby.

My blanket in place, Apollo was able to draw himself up and look me in the eye. We must resolve this situation, he said, or we will take more serious steps.

I won't pay for something I didn't do, you little peckerwood.

Must you be so insulting?

I must.

You're a mean person, if you'll forgive me saying so.

My saying so. It's called a gerund, fuckwit. Instead of hassling me with obviously doctored photos, you could spend a few hours reading a grammar textbook, since you're in such a Position of Authority.

Sir, I must insist—

Whatever he insisted, it was to my closed door. I suspect I showed him I'm not someone to be trifled with. Of course, I am worried about ramifications. It was hard enough to find this hovel. I'm not at all sure where I'd go if he actually threw me out. Still, it wouldn't be the first time I've been kicked out. Ask them.

No, not *her*. The first them. Yeah, yeah, yeah.

Woolton

We started almost by accident. In the beginning, there was Rob and there was me. We were neighbors, friends. He played drums. I played nothing but wanted to. Barry came later, a friend of a friend, and found and brought in Leon a year later. It was us four, but it could have just easily been any other four. It didn't much matter. Only the *four* of it mattered. Fidelity to the originals. To the illusion.

I was sixteen.

We needed a bassist, and I figured bass was the easiest to learn, so that was me. Spent a hundred bucks for my first bass. I couldn't afford an amp, so we ran it through a stereo speaker, the grate rattling with every note. It didn't matter how bad it sounded since I couldn't play yet. Didn't stop us from setting up in my family garage and going to town.

Barry taught me a few notes, enough to stumble through a number. That whole first summer spent learning one song, twisting and shouting all afternoon long. The neighbors must have loved us. It didn't matter. I couldn't have cared less. I loved every moment.

Earlier that year, a schoolmate had handed me a cassette tape. *The red album*, she called it. Check it out, it will change everything, she promised. She was right.

Click. Press. Hiss.

Fucking momentous. Who knew?

I sat in my bedroom alone, always alone, turned it up and listened. No drug ever got me as high. I was such a fool, I had *no idea*. At once I perceived each song's simultaneity and separateness. The coalescing of notes, chords, bass, drums, licks, strums, harmonies, movement, so much movement, and heart. All of that heart, heart I'd been missing, an IV straight into my ventricles. Such a neat, bright line drawn between the before and the after, what was and what was to come. I levitated, sailed away, floated on magic harmonies that seemed written only for me. Transformed.

Boots

Yet I was nothing and I knew it. But I could slip on another skin and all at once seem to be *more*. I knew I needed the right guitar, my cheap hundred dollar bass would never do. I got wind of a clerk at the local record store who was selling a Höfner. I wheedled my old man, whined ceaselessly until the cheap bastard finally fronted me the $250 so I'd shut up and go away. I handed the stringy-haired clerk his fistful of cash and he slid the chipboard case toward me. I opened the clasps and there it was. My Höfner. I carefully picked it up, noticed how light it was. (I hadn't known then they were hollow bodies. Fucking perfect, right?) I sat down with it and positioned it to cover my erection. I knew what a leap forward this was. I was already *better*. I could see the glow in Leon's and Barry's eyes. My place was secure at last. I was legit, don't fuck with me. A week later, the three of us hopped the subway turnstile and headed across town, where rumor was a shop carried knockoff pleather Chelsea boots with Cuban heels. At fifty-five dollars, they were a fortune, but the minute I slipped them on, I felt taller, cooler, better. I didn't take them off until they disintegrated a year and a half later, until the smell finally drove even me away.

Fishing

This morning, I woke to an envelope slid under my door. A cheaply photocopied form letter on faded FBI letterhead. You are requested in person, it read, at the FBI Field Office on such and such a day at such and such a time. You may bring an attorney. Failure to comply will result in blood curdling punishments. Your mama wears combat boots. No mention of the senator or Bowtie. Smells of a fishing expedition. *They got nuthin'*, as DeNiro's Capone once roared. I crumple the summons and throw in in the trash, a brave gesture performed for an audience of one.

Practice

It's the third time we've gone through this song, and at the same part, Barry improvises a harmony that isn't on the original. The first two times he does it, Leon and I exchange an eyeroll, but this time, I stop playing and turn on Barry.

"What the fuck? You sound like an idiot."

We're a year in and we've gotten better. We're signed up for a Battle of the Bands night at an upcoming fan convention, The Festival, it's called. We're trying to learn a showstopper or two, dreams of winning the night. High stakes.

Barry is surprised by my rage. So am I. It takes him a moment to absorb his confusion before he can convert it to anger. In the caesura, I hear Rob and Leon fiddling with their instruments. At last, Barry steps to.

"Fuck you."

Really? *Fuck you?* I'm disappointed by the paucity of his imagination. I was hoping for more. I'm always hoping for more. It makes me angrier.

"Don't improvise, okay? If it's not on the original record, don't fucking do it. How hard can that be?"

"Relax. It sounds cool. No one will care."

"It doesn't sound cool. It sounds obvious. If it was cool, *they* would have done it that way."

Leon steps in, the peacemaker. "It's fine, let's just try it again. It's getting better."

He counts off, and we run through the number. Barry is sufficiently abashed not to try it again. I should feel victorious, but I don't. I envy him, and I think he knows it. I'm crap with harmony, can't hold a counterpoint line, am almost always drawn back to the melody, like a short bus moth to the light. It's like my brain can't register a second but equal thing occupying the same space; I just hear the boldest lines. It's been a problem since the beginning, and they've had to change up the arrangements to cover up this defect in me. My voice has an acceptable range, but it's thin and reedy and cracks at the highest registers I'm expected to hit. At first, I loved the camaraderie of the thing, sitting around with my friends, with instruments, trying to figure out how to make some noise. It was a good time, until they got better and I didn't.

Studio Two

Sometimes I would imagine what it must have been like to have been one of *them*. No, that's not right. I would imagine I *was* one of them. Sitting in that studio, major recording session, eyeball to eyeball as we make music history. Late nights, cigarette butts, laughter, experiments. No idea too off the wall—backward guitar licks! sped-up pianos! electronic feedback! Everything is possible. The miracle of getting there first, everything is brand new. I sometimes imagine those glorious chords coming out from *my* fingers. Sitting at that Steinway in Studio Two, singing the guys a rough take of my latest as I drift away into this sublimely happy place of pure melody. For a moment, I'm happy. For a moment, I believe that love really is all you need. For a moment, I believe it's me.

Lark

Leon and I are sharing a smoke outside after practice. A few doors down, behind a neighbor's fence so his folks won't see us. He's my best friend, and these are my favorite moments. He's short, intense. Messes with his hair for hours to get it just so. I sense that he's smarter than I am, or more worldly at least. He passes me the cigarette. Lark, the brand they smoked. I don't inhale, don't know how, but I can make it look good. Sometimes we talk about girls. On this day, Leon sports a hickey the size of a flattened grape. I introduced him to my friend Karen, who I always liked, and now they're rutting like feral cats. But he's my best friend, and that's how it goes sometimes. We're not talking about girls, though. He's giving me that side-eye that usually precedes some bit of criticism.

"Why do you get so angry at Barry?"

I take another drag and hand him back his cigarette. "Because he's so fucking annoying. He ruins the songs. It's so fucking arrogant, who is he to add stuff to those songs?" They're perfect. Leon nods but seems unpersuaded. He smokes some more, thinks a bit. We sit together, suspended in affectionate silence.

Why do you get so angry at Barry?
Because I've seen the way the others look at me and each other when I can't quite hit a high note or when I lose the harmony line.

Why do you get so angry at Barry?
Because he sucks and he's still better than I am. I don't say it, but we all know it.

Bowtie (2)

This morning, a light dusting of snow. Bowtie remains inconveniently alive.

Had a false start there as another of his brethren, a corpulent and repellent right-wing shock jock finally succumbed to a long overdue aneurysm. His decampment from this mortal coil brought me only muted celebration, as I spent far too many hours gaming out how Nevsky's hand might be detected in all this. A sort of swing at one and hit the other type of calisthenics. But it was a forced exercise; Nevsky has yet to act. I tell myself he is biding his time, looking for his moment. That it's only a matter of time until he strikes. But my confidence has begun to flag. Perhaps Nevsky is just another disappointment, like the rest of them. First time was a fluke, a happy coincidence but when the time came to stand and be counted…

Christ, I do go on.

I consider messaging him directly, asking for a progress update. But any direct contact between us will surely be used against me later, collected by my new admirers from the FBI as evidence of a criminal conspiracy. No, for now, I simply have to wait and trust—two things I have never mastered.

Is the noise all there is?

Next door, the elephants come and go, talking of Michelangelo.

Pete

Leon's friend, our first hanger-on. An entourage of one. Pete shows up toward the end of that first year. We've gotten tighter. With a lot of practice, and with my slipshod vocals relegated to backing lines, we almost sound like them. But we realize we need a utility player, especially if we want to take home the big prize. There are simply too many instruments, harmonies, musical lines. We need someone who can add that fifth voice, can keep the tambourine steady, even pluck out a line on the piano. Pete is eager to please.

He is tall, handsome, talented, and kind, and I'm immediately threatened. He sits in on all our rehearsals, leaping happily to his feet when he has a job to do. His voice is sweet and smooth, aching and pure at the highest registers. We use him more and more, usually at my expense. One day, I come back in from my smoke break, and he is handling my Höfner. I'd be less angry coming upon him fucking my girlfriend, if I had one. It's usurpation, vile and violating. I catch them mid-refrain, running through one of our battle of the band numbers. Just having some fun, they assure me. Killing the time.

Mutherfucker is even left-handed. I don't think it's possible to hate someone more than I do in this moment. I grab my guitar, shove his tambourine hard at him. Stay in your lane, biatch. We start up again. I count off.
(uh-one two three FAWR!)

Three true facts:

Uh-one:	Pete is way more talented than I am.
Two:	It's a good thing I started this band.
Three:	Boots don't make the man.

Fawr?

Pointers

This morning, I received a message via the dating website. Subject line: Pointers?

Hello there. A strange profile, yours. Iceberg-like, I think, hiding a lot under the water. As it happens, I've been having a hard time finding my way as well and welcome any pointers—what did you do today to make the world a little bit better? I'm open to suggestion. Best, Emma. PS Coldplay ugh

My habit is to delete these but there's something in this message that catches me, reminds me, just a bit around the edges, of my wife, faint but enough to keep me reading. Unguarded, honest. Earnest. I stare at Emma's message for hours. I write seventeen different replies and delete them all. They range from snark to mock profundity to terse mystery. Dripping with bullshit, each of them a pose. In the end, I settle for brief and honest which, in my hands, is also a pose:

Hello there.
Steer clear.

An hour later, I send this:
World-improving pro-tip: Remember to wash your recycling.

An hour after that, I send this:
Coldplay: The early stuff doesn't make me want to ingest my own vomit.

An hour after that, I send this:
The word iceberg is a partial loan translation from the Dutch word *ijsberg*, literally meaning ice mountain, cognate to Danish *isbjerg*, German Eisberg, Low Saxon *Iesbarg* and Swedish *isberg*.

I am still sending replies many hours later, pounding without cease on my keyboard, when I notice her account has been deleted.

Ficus

Battle of the Bands. Dingy roadside chain hotel ballroom. Thick with fans, music nerds, getalifers. T-shirts, buttons, swag bags. Squeals and shrieks. The other bands have been solid enough, but I like our chances. We're congregated on the side of the stage with all the other acts when the emcee calls our name.

As I start to climb the stage, Barry and Leon stand shoulder to shoulder, blocking me. I don't understand, think they are messing with me.

"Very funny. Let's go!"

They look at one another and Leon shakes his head. He presses his fingertips against my chest, holding me back.

"Sorry. Not you."

What comes next never dawns on me, though it should have.

"We're making a change." Barry nods in Pete's direction. He stands there, suited up and ready to go. Holding a left-handed Höfner. I feel like I'm staring into a mirror at my more talented self, my might-have-been self. Barry and Leon hold me in place as Pete worms past them and climbs the stage. Once he's plugged into his amp, they release me and follow. Rob pulls up the rear, a sad and shameful look on his face. I teeter backward, dizzy, about to collapse. My eyes on the ground. Who has seen this? Who has witnessed my humiliation? Miles away, I hear them count down (uh-one two three FAWR!), hear the music begin. For a few bars, I am frozen with shock and confusion. Finally, I bolt from the stage, out the hall, down the stairs, into the street, running as fast as I can, guitar flapping on my back, eyes blinded with tears until I find a bush—ficus, I believe, snow dusted—and vomit into it.

A (Partial) List of Things Lost:

My first fountain pen. My father's pinky ring. Spiderman Issue 122. Every house key, at some time or another. Fancy sunglasses. My nerve. Cheap sunglasses. Swiss army knife. Them. (No disaster.) Die cast race car (Corvette). Love letters. First, third and sixth cell phones. Perspective. My first driver's license. Report cards. All the goddamned sunglasses. *barryleonrob*

Four Shitweasels

They won that night, Pete and the boys.

I was sick for days afterward. Waves of anxiety, rage, and nausea twisted me around like some deranged, feral puppet. I couldn't eat. The smell of food nauseated me. Anger gave way to depression which soon flared back up into anger. Would I mope, depleted and weak, or would I fight, furious and formidable? How to counter this enormous betrayal? Leon tried to call, came by in person, even wrote a letter to explain that it wasn't personal, that we could carry on as friends. I didn't care about any of it, didn't want to hear it, he was dead to me.

They were right, of course. I knew it then, I know it now. I would have done the same.

But facts is facts and rage is rage, and now I had four new shitweasels to hate. The Drab Four. The Scab Four.

Never played one of those fucking albums again.

Simulacrum

Years later, I tracked Pete down online. He lives in Arizona, still plays in a cover band, if you can believe it. CPA during the week. On the weekends he slathers his fat ass in Crisco and squeezes his extra pounds into his Sargeant Pepper costume and plays pool halls and county fairs. I watch his videos and can almost smell the BBQ smoking in the background. Sonofabitch still sounds pretty good, but I find the spectacle pathetic. Once, perhaps, there was something pleasantly escapist about the illusion, pretending it was them. Now it's just a group of dadbod white guys locked into their one-way nostalgia trip. Anemic screams from the moms in the audience, who know the role they are expected to play but can't quite seem to embrace the indignity of it all. Hours of footage on YouTube, though who would watch any of it when the originals are right there is beyond me. Still, he racks up the views.

What really galls me is how happy he seems. It's that same kind of unearned bliss I see in WillyBee. Are they too stupid to realize how *inappropriate* their joy is to the moment? This infantile escapism, an inability to look the horrors of the age square in the face and understand that the only sane posture is one of fury. And action. What is fucking wrong with these people?

Laughter

Here is some of what I learned today, having spent an entire afternoon with a glass pressed against the wall, listening to the elephants, trying to untangle this latest FBI mystery.

First, I learned that the whole listening-through-a-glass thing is movie bullshit that does nothing in real life.

Second, I hear… laughter.

At first, I assume it's directed at me. That seems the most logical interpretation. What other possible reason could they have for happiness in their reduced state, five of them crammed into this cold, peeling bedsit, this open sore of a flat, this festering abscess waiting to suck us all into the ground? It can only be my predicament that amuses them.

Yet as the hours pass, I don't hear anything about me. Not a veiled reference to be found. They seem to enjoy each other, amuse each other. I catch fragments of things, pablum about better tomorrows and temporary setbacks. Platitudes from motivational posters—always darkest before the dawn kind of banal claptrap. Shallow, empty thinking. And still, they laugh. What do they know? I wonder, shivering.

Zen

I read all of her posts in WillyBee's message boards. She's diligent about getting her work done and turned in on time, doesn't miss a deadline. Her thoughts are clear, orderly, sincere enough. She obviously takes the exercise seriously. But there's something off, something only I can see.

They're dutiful, as though she knows what she is supposed to be saying and feeling. But it's all a bit rote. Like something within her is extinguished. My foul handiwork. Perhaps she thinks this sustained bout of walking the talk will reinvigorate her, bring her battered soul flaring back to life. She's always been an optimist.

She took me to a Zen Garden once. Me. Keep an open mind, she said, which I took to be a bit of Zen humor. We stood together in the shade of a giant cypress, and I stared at the swept gravel, followed the undulations and swirls and briefly felt myself disappearing into the patterns, into a glimpse of other possibilities, the other mes I might have been in any other life if only I hadn't always been so stubbornly me in this one.

This is stupid. Let's go.

She shook her head, held me to the spot. Just look. Follow the lines. Don't think so much. So I tried. And I loved her and I hated her for believing in my possibilities. Too much to live up to, you know? Of course you do, tweeps.

The laughing next door has stopped. A respectful moment of silence. I know whose side they're on.

Look at Me

WillyBee is "concerned." I haven't been doing my homework. He sends me solicitous messages. How can he support me on my journey?

Support *this*, you inbred wanker.

WillyBee, I have decided, is not for me. I chalk it up to the indignity of homework but truth is I can't bear to see her like this. Still, I blame the homework. To my surprise, WillyBee offers me a free one-on-one session to work it through. This I recognize as a premium offering; this capitalist ass rapist normally charges $1500 for the pleasure of his one-on-one. I'm suspicious, of course—what's his next MLM Ponzi move? How does this talk trap me into an endless cycle of WillyBee seminars and throw pillows? But I take the bait, if only for the pleasure of telling him to kiss off in person.

I never get the chance. I have underestimated him, there's no doubt. He sees straight through my shit, like he has some mystical third forehead eye. Doesn't break the slightest sweat in nailing me cold. You're not on a silent retreat, he tells me; and you're not doing your work. You're so angry, so bitter, it comes through the Zoom, even in your silence, even through your total self-negation. A cloud of rage. That's what you are. So cut the crap and turn on your camera and look at me.

Look at me.

My heart thuds like a pair of bass drums, and I don't remember the movement of my finger to click the camera on but suddenly there we are, Santa Claus and the Devil, staring it out, eyeball to eyeball. He pets his little doggy all Blofeld-like, and I wait for him to deliver the death blow, say whatever it is he has planned that will take me out, put in my place. The super-villain speech, that reliable set piece. Instead, he asks me a question. With incomparable sadness and what looks like compassion but I dismiss as pity:

What made you like this?

How do you explain *thumbsthumbsthumbs*?

Instead, I know exactly when and why my finger clicks this time. FyoDos has left the building.

ELVIS VOICE
Thankyouverymuch.

Goldfish

Fuck that poseur WillyBee, I've still got thumbsthumbsthumbs after all. Yet whether I log on for a few minutes or a few hours, the hopelessness sets in at once, an IV of dread jacked right into the brain stem. There's literally nothing for me here except this roiling sea of rage, and still I keep coming back for more even though I know I will never find any answers here, that every visit makes me dumber, makes me meaner. There's not a jot of wisdom to found here, just a sea of hipper than thou bullshit. You trot out all the bits of cultural debris polluting your brain, the more obscure, the better, and you piss them into the wind hoping to keep the splashback to a minimum. Any single sentence out of context can look profound. Or ironic. Or knowing. Or all three at once. It's a showman's paradise, and it's a razor blade ride to madness.

The worst thing, though, is I can't remember *anything*. Nothing registers any more. Every thought, even the furious ones, especially the furious ones, get washed away like footprints in sand. Sometimes, as I lie awake until dawn's approach, I have these intricate, shimmering, brilliant ideas, spinning inside my brain. I lose myself in the elegance of my conceptions. Then I sit up to write them down, and I can't remember a word. Each round of rage becomes a weird new rebirth, a goldfish traversing its bowl. (How she loved Goldfish as a kid, the only thing she'd eat for days, I remember *that*.) My brain can no longer store anything new, everything merely passes through on its way to somewhere else, somewhere better. I live outside myself, and I feel myself vanishing, and somewhere some part of me is sure that if only—

—Right there, just now. Had it. A glimpse, a reflection in the rearview. And now it's gone.

Also: I "forgot" to go to the FBI office today. Knight takes rook.

Bowtie (3)

Well, well, well. Bowtie has gone missing. Did not show up to tape his show last week, the first time he's missed a broadcast since he slithered up from hell's ninth ring. No trace of him at home. Cell phone in his house. Car in the driveway. No signs of disturbance or violence. It's possible that he's slipped back to the netherworld where he belongs, but we both know that's not the case, comrade.

My heart is trying to break free of my rib cage. I find myself imagining his torture for hours. Graphic mental footage as Nevsky hooks a car battery to Bowtie's minuscule manly bits. I pull down my sheet of Those Who Must Die and begin prioritizing them, an activity that takes me hours. It's not quite so easy to rank one's hatreds. Who goes first? What if Nevsky is caught or if his devotion to me flags before he finishes? Who are the ones who simply must go first? So much to do.

Waterloo

Apollo has served me with a seven day "pay or quit" notice. Game on.

It sits on my desk, pulsing. Hot and threatening. I don't want to touch it for fear of burning my fingers. The three hundred bucks itself is trivial. It's not about the money. It's about the capitulation. Never fuckin' surrender, that's what the old stogie-chomper would say. Fight on the beaches and all that crap. I should have seen this coming.

Something has shifted a bit with Bowtie's disappearance. It's as though I can feel the gentle pressure of Nevsky's fingertips at my back, nudging me forward and out the door. Time to step to. Put on some clothes and stare down that manbunned piece of shit who is trying to ruin my peace.

It's a long walk up the stairs to his office, made longer by the nausea, the racing of my heart, the rehearsing in my brain of my carefully crafted devastating riposte. I know this is our Waterloo. Only one of us will come out the other side. I stand before his door, collecting my nerves, raise my hand to knock, my hand freezes, suspended. I'm prepared. I'm in the right. He's shit. I'm ready. Yet I can't knock. I'm flooded with my own cowardice. I think of Nevsky, the senator, Bowtie, WallyBee, *mydadissuchanasshole* and my hand floats there, unmoving, unknocking. I can feel the impulse to lower it, to step back, to turn away and slink back to my room. I'm about to surrender when I hear the murmur of voices in his office. For some reason, the thought of an audience buoys me, gives me a reason to go through with confronting Apollo in a way he is unlikely to forget. I knock. The voices stop. I knock again and open the door, not waiting for an invitation. Nevsky would be proud.

The air in his office is thick with marijuana smoke. Apollo sits on a ratty couch with two of his pals. His eyes are glazed. He glances up at me, sees the notice in my hand, which I throw at his feet. I'm all set to go, ready to deliver my peroration, when the little shit begins to giggle. His friends are shifting awkwardly, and I recognize them at last as the FBI agents who knocked on my door. They aren't feds at all, a pair of flesh dildos in Black Flag punk T-shirts fellating a bong the size of a Buick between them. They exchange an indifferent look, shrug at me and begin to laugh and laugh. Apollo joins them and their rising chorus of laughter drowns out my prepared remarks, drowns out my fury, my indignation, my helplessness.

Kermit

There's a popular animated GIF of Kermit the Frog, shaking his arms with wild abandon. It's commonly used by people to indicate excessive excitement about something.

I think they've all got it wrong.

The frog is losing his shit.

Acrostic

Light Induced Zebra Accelerator
Liquid Interior Zamboni Assistant
Lavender Influenced Zen Acrobatics
Limbic Inchoate Zombie Aroma
Lackadasical Intermediary Ziggurat Aspirations
Leeward Instrumental Zeitgeist Appropriator
Loquacious Inveterate Zygote Assimilation

I got a million of 'em…

(Won't say it, can't make me.)

Consolation

High school English, sophomore year. Ms. Finnegan made us memorize this one:

> *Bred to a harder thing*
> *Than Triumph, turn away*
> *And like a laughing string*
> *Whereon mad fingers play*
> *Amid a place of stone,*
> *Be secret and exult,*
> *Because of all things known*
> *That is most difficult.*

Damn right it is. I remember this now, as I think of Apollo. Be secret and exult. Yep, yep, yep. This one feels like it was written for me. To me. It's from a poem called "To a Friend Whose Work Has Come to Nothing," which is pretty spot on, could be my mission statement. Sometimes I imagine if I had really listened to this poem years ago, before she left, before they left, before I blew everything up with my one-way ticket to Fucksburg, that it might maybe have slowed me down, diverted me off this trajectory of fury. I mean, isn't that all anyone really needs—to be consoled?

Still. The guy he wrote this for died on the *Lusitania*. So, you know, well done Yeats. I had a point when I started. I'm sure of it.

Monomorium minimum

Take one:

It was a nice house, small but with room for all three of us. A bit tatty in the corners but bright and cheerful. You could hear the waves in the backyard, smell the salt tang of the nearby bay. Seagulls (*seabirds of the family Laridae in the suborder Lari*) crooning pre-dawn. There were struggles, we struggled, I was struggling. Already unemployed, subsisting on her largesse. The kid withdrawing into her cocoon of misery. But we were together, and the sun broke through most days. Perhaps it all would have held together, but for the ants. *Et in Arcadia, ego.*

They first showed up following a rainstorm. This wasn't unusual. I could understand the damp little bastards seeking out a bit of shelter from the deluge. But that spring, they didn't leave. They kept showing up, marching through the kitchen, the bathroom, the bedroom. It wasn't an infestation, just a few intrepid scouts blazing a trail, on the hunt for dinner. Sometimes I'd squish them with my thumb. Sometimes with a paper towel. Sometimes I'd spray water and flush them down the drain. Then she explained to me that the dying ants were sending out some kind of chemical distress signal to the tribe, which would bring them around in greater number. I could see what she was doing, trying to give me a transactional, self-beneficial reason to stop doing the thing she knew was wrong—killing them. I'd mock her, roll my eyes as she scooped the individual ants on a bit of card stock and shook them off outside in the yard. That little bastard is coming straight back in, I said. Where was the deterrence? She patted my arm gently. They're social. They have colonies. They're just trying to eat. They don't know it's our house. I shrugged and sulked, diminished yet again in the glow of her moral superiority, which I both loved and hated. I continued to squish the little bastards when she wasn't around, and they continued their march through our kitchen throughout the spring and into early summer.

Foreplay

This, she once joked, would be the ultimate Dirty Sex Talk™ for me:

Oh baby, you're so right, baby, you're right, you're always right baby, my god you're so right, oh your big, bad rightness feels sooooo good…

I mean, I *think* she was joking. We never got around to trying. Some nights, though, my thoughts drift off, imagination takes hold and…

Oh, puh-lease.

Only Connect

I've been watching Pete's videos again, another YouTube all-nighter. I shouldn't, but there's something that compels me to return. Maybe it's the mistakes he makes. They are few and far between, but they are there, we both know it. He's not so damn perfect. A dropped note from a tricky bass line. A fudged lyric. Perhaps I watch to content myself with his fallibility.

There's something else, though. I feel absurd saying it aloud, it's a such nascent thought, barely a glimmer of something that arrives in the deepest still of the night, but as I watch him play, there's a little whisper in the back of my brain, a tickle that won't go away…

Nevsky?

It's crazy, of course, I know it is. I don't *seriously* consider it. But I do kick at it idly, like a sparrow's corpse in the road. Strange connections. Little things. Mostly just that air of confidence. He has no love of Bowtie, that's clear from his social media. He cracks the occasional joke about the missing commentator, but it's pretty anodyne stuff, there's much worse out there. Which could simply be a brilliant cover. This is the thing about life amid these webs, you begin to connect. See the joins that everyone else misses, the secret things that explain the workings of the universe. So of course it's ridiculous to contemplate that my overweight ersatz jobbing soundalike moonlights as @NevskySoldier, slayer of demons. But I'm looking through you, mutherfucker.

Louboutin

Years before any of this, I was sitting in a park breaking up with a woman in agonizing fits and starts. Or she was breaking up with me, we never fully sorted it out. It had been that kind of relationship since the beginning, neither fully in, nor fully out. But we both could feel the air leaving the balloon at last, and so we sat on a park bench, fumbling through how to let each other go with a scrap of dignity. We fell into a companionable silence as we followed a roly poly bug making its slow, effortful way across the path, inching toward the safety of the far grass. We watched the passersby who were heedless of the existential struggle playing out under their heels. We flinched with each close call, gripped each other's hands in anticipation, in dread. And just as he heroically reached the fringes of the grass, execution by Louboutin. The poor little bastard curled into a dying ball and we took that as our sign from the gods to part company. Every word of this is true.

Monomorium minimum (2)

Once more, with feeling:

By summer, the ants had swarmed. Despite every effort to be clean and lock food down, the word had gotten around ant circles; this was the place to be. I was repelled by what was now an infestation, repelled by their little insect bodies making forays toward my meals, tracking god knows what kind of virulent infections into my grub. She called me a drama queen, a favorite epithet even then. I researched traps, found one that would have the worker ants transport the poison back into the colony and wipe it out, which I found admirably efficient. She was horrified. Put her foot down. No fucking way. She didn't swear a lot, and when she did, one took notice. She told me she wasn't going to countenance ant genocide to spare my delicate sensibilities. The kid snickered from her bedroom. The fact is, I admired her moral rectitude, and it turned me on ever so slightly that I would push and push and push, and she wouldn't yield. It was the supreme negative capability moonwalk move: I wanted her to resist, would lose all respect if she yielded, yet I wanted to be right, wanted to win. Wanted her to cry uncle.

One night, while she was asleep, I hid a couple of the Antschwitz traps in the kitchen. When I stumbled out for coffee that morning, she'd already found them, was holding them under my nose, her face rigid with fury. They are *alive*, she reminded me. They are *social*. They are just doing what they programmed to do, what is in their nature.

So am I, Lavender Influenced Zen Acrobatics, so am I.

Don't *ever* do it again, she warned. I'd forgotten a basic truth: she was smarter than I was. I hung my head, defeated. *Ants, 1. Me, Zero.* That should have been the end of it.

Arrears

Apollo at my door again, this time with muscle. He has affixed a 72-hour quit notice on my door. I hear him fiddling with the paperwork, so I swing the door open to confront him. Due to my unpaid debt, if I do not vacate, I will be forcibly removed. He inclines his head in the direction of his gorilla: Crew cut. Brawny with the smell of ex-military on him. Boring ass *semper fi* tattoo. A cliché but more than up to the job. He's unfazed by my nakedness. Apollo advises me that only immediate full payment to settle my arrears will stop this proceeding. Otherwise, that's that. He holds himself erect, his bloodshot eye contact unwavering, full of that smug dignity of his that makes me want to slap the shit out of him.

I go full Kermit on him.

I stand there shrieking at him, sweat-soaked and pale, calling him "my executioner" and promising to kill him some day. Charley pokes his head out of his front door, drawn by the ruckus, and soon his whole clan is observing with worried eyes as my foam-flecked tirade continues. Apollo simply stands there, arms folded, impassive, and I finally dart back into my room, junk flapping, and collect the payment from my mattress along with the elephants' tattered doormat. I return to the hallway and hurl it all at Apollo IT'S MONEY YOU FUCKING WANT WELL THERE YOU ARE YOU STONER PRICK NOW LEAVE ME IN FUCKING PEACE and as he bends down with a sigh to collect the bills I piss on them, I know I shouldn't but when you gotta go, you gotta go, and there's a point of principle to be made here. His gorilla looks askance at my dick, unimpressed, but I piss my angry Niagara onto his pile of dough undeterred and I slam the door behind me bellowing PAID IN FULL, YOU MUTHER-FUCKIN' MAGGOT.

Fugue

I return to my room, shaking. A vision takes place, and I give myself over to it. I imagine Apollo on the ground, scooping up my money. Only now I place my foot on this throat, trapping him. He flails, terrified, scrabbling at my foot, but I don't budge. He looks up me, abject, with pleading eyes. I lean into it, press more weight on his throat. I watch his eyes bulge with fear, disbelief, pain. I could let him go, lesson learned, but I'm too far gone. I stomp, bringing down my full weight, and hear the sharp crack of his splintering neck. His eyes drain out and he goes still. I'm sickened, enervated, yet I vibrate with a palpable electricity. It always happens this way, these fever dreams that I can't stop, they unspool like some demonic short feature. Then it's over, and I step out of this fugue state feeling sickened, horrified at what I've just seen, appalled at what I am capable of. Because I am, right? Capable? Thoughts are deeds, no matter what the rabbis say. And then I just want to die. I'm irretrievably polluted. Contaminated. Deformed and degraded, barely human. I was not like this before, I'm fairly certain. This shitsite has ruined me, my constant immersion in the hatreds that run through my feed, an accelerant to madness. I might have had a chance without it, a lifetime of petty resentments, to be sure, but manageable with therapy, drugs, self-delusion, family. But this is something far worse. I am more Nevsky that I realized. *Will to power*, you feel me?

Charley (2)

It's the morning after my shrieking pissing contest with Apollo, and the elephants hustle away quietly, but I hear them move out, feel the urgent rustle of their departure. I peek into the hallway as the back of Charley's blond curls vanish from view, hurried away by his anxious mother. He tries to look back and wave, but she blocks him, speeds him up the stairs, away from me.

All quiet now. No more laughing. Nobody here now but us chickens.

Monomorium minimum (3)

Third time's the charm:

The ant invasion continued into autumn. I had returned to the occasional surreptitious ant homicide, more protest move than meaningful response. We lapsed into an uneasy detente, the ants and I, mostly ignoring one another, until October, when my birthday cake was consumed.

It was a bespoke beauty, Valrhona chocolate (my favorite), and even the kid roused herself from her torpor to help out, garnishing the edges with icing renderings of her favorite animated game characters. It was meant to be a surprise, was left out on the counter just briefly to come to room temperature. Which is when Rommel Ant and his troops made their move. I came out to find the cake engulfed in a swirling black cloud. Battalions of reinforcements streaming in from three directions, flanking and throttling. I was outnumbered, the battle already lost. Yet in my fevered derangement, I saw not ants but perceived instead a kind of maggoty dismemberment taking place. They were spilling out of the crevices in the cake, pulsing, oozing. I plunged my hands into the cake, tore it apart to reveal an entire seething colony within. I began to shout, and I hurled the cake to the ground, dashing it to bits.

They came running in, frightened by the sound. I begin to scream *It's them or me* like a lunatic. I slaughtered hundreds of them, smashing wide swaths flat with my palms, which I then held under her nose smeared with chocolate and ant corpses, still screaming *It's them or me*. I expected her rage, her anger over all the needless ant dismemberment, her core philosophy violated.

Instead, she puts her arms around me in a tearful embrace. We sink down to the ground together, and she strokes my hair as I gnash and sob in her arms. Even the kid comes over and puts a tentative, frightened hand on my shoulder. It's a peace offering, a moment to set it on a different path, to maybe just maybe move forward. So much kindness and compassion and worry and *I'm not fucking worth it.*

The traps. I want the traps. My voice is adamantine. It contains no room, not an inch. It's the line I will never be able to undraw.

The traps. Or I go.

Her eyes fill with tears and her embrace loosens just a hitch but I feel it, register the slackening and I know I've won and I've lost. She nods, wipes her tears, and leaves me on the floor. I put out the traps. I've kept them since the spring, waiting for this moment. But an hour later, she comes through and throws them all out. I'm sorry, she says. I just can't. I don't press the point, it doesn't matter because she is good and decent and cares about LIFE and yet she has cried uncle and now I'm truly broken, defeated, because it's all just as bad as I think it is and I hate myself more than I can find words for and all this hatred has to go somewhere do something and so there's nothing for it but *thumbsthumbsthumbs* so by the time I depart a week later, I've already left them. And that's when the cold sets in, this infernal cold that never leaves me.

Dumpster Fire

I stand in front of a dumpster in the alley, its lid thrown open, its maw gaping in expectation. I'm trembling as I hold my laptop and my phone over it, sending the signal to my brain to release them, to let them fall in, once and for all. I imagine leaping flames singing my hands—there's never a raging dumpster fire when you actually need one—and still I can't release them. I stand there screaming, shrieking really, convulsing like a madman with a seizure, awash with spit and sweat and snot and blood and tears and just GO AWAY FUCK YOU ALL GODDAMNIT JUST GO LEAVE ME ALONE AND DIE DIE DIE and still my grip won't loosen. What have I become? Save. Me.

We go inside, the three of us, this unhappy family, spent. Apollo withdraws into his office, pale, as we cross the lobby, but I feel no triumph. I feel nothing at all.

Bowtie (4)

This morning, on my pillow: a bowtie, flecked with blood.

At least, I think so. Come nightfall, I can't find it anywhere.

(I mean, who are you gonna believe? Me or your lyin' eyes?)

Act Two Turning Point

New information today, how could I have missed it? Bowtie was in Dallas when he disappeared. (Still no sign of that foul little asslicker. I imagine him decomposing in a dumpster behind a rodeo bar somewhere.)

Thing is, the same day, Pete was in Dallas. With his band. Playing a gig.

Right? You see it, too.

I started messaging him this morning. *We have to talk. Call me. Email me.* I sent dozens, no reply. I can see he's reading them, but he refuses to engage. He thinks I want to blame him, doesn't realize I want to thank him. To praise him for this majestic tribute he seems to be paying me. (I'm still hard-pressed to come up with *why*. The only thing I can think of is this is an expiation of his lifelong regret over his monstrous betrayal. That holds together, more or less.)

So there's only one move left. Time to be bold, once again.

Pete and his band are playing next week at that very same fan convention from all those years ago. He's graduated from Battle of the Bands to the headline act of the weekend, so it seems only logical for me to rise up out of this basement, make my way over and look right in his fucking eyes and say *I know what you did. I see you.*

It's an alarming prospect, being back in the world, but the fact is that Apollo has ruined my hovel, befouled it with the stink of his sneering sanctimony. I don't know if this place was ever home, but it's certainly not home any longer. And it pains me to admit things have gotten too quiet since Charley's brood moved out. Is it possible that I miss them? The prospect appalls me. So, it seems the next thing to do is pack my gear, get dressed, leave this room, and face the meatscape.

Missives

Dear Pete,

True story, one I don't think you know. I almost gave you my Höfner that day. You know which day, don't be coy. It was clear to me that you deserved it more than I did, that you'd do more with it, and I nearly handed it over to you right then and there. Sure, I was livid but I'm a stone-cold realist, and I know when I'm beaten. And keeping it around would just torture me, a metonym for this long fucking failed life. Speaking of which, I've left it to you in my will. Couldn't think of anyone better, and you'd actually appreciate and even maybe care for it. Which is all we can ever ask, right? I do wish you'd reply to any one of these pings. No recriminations, just talk. There's this thing now, and it's bigger than us both, isn't it? I know it's you, right? It has to be. I understand you need to keep mum, lay low, take a powder. I just need to know we are on the same page here, marching in unison, if you will, toward something together. So don't be too shocked if I pop by, just to say hello. How will you greet me, I wonder? With openness? With humility and friendship? With stern purpose? With perhaps a soupçon of shame? I guess that's on you, action man. Me, I got a bus to catch. See you when I see you.

P.S. You do realize you're playing the last verse in the medley wrong, don't you? He obviously double-tracked the original bass line, you're missing like half of it. Don't get sloppy and lazy in your old age, okay? I see you.

(I put the piss in epistolary.)

But it seems to us we might as well stop here...

Choices

"However, the 'notes' of this paradoxalist don't end here. He couldn't resist and kept on writing. But it also seems to us that we might as well stop here."

That's where Fyodor ends it. I get it, it's a witty and elegant turn in its way. The narrator continues to rant despite himself, powerless to shut the fuck up. But because we, the wise reader, know it's just more of the same, why not tune out then and there? Perhaps he's ranting still, to this very day, locked in his St. Petersburg basement, somewhere out of time, unaware that the world has moved on without him. That's the risk, isn't it? The isolation of our bubble, the belief that this space we're trapped in represents the whole of the world.

Me, I'd have liked to have seen what happened next. Where he went from there. Where I go. Where we all go. Because it can't end fucking here, not like this. It just can't. So, what are the choices?

Up and out, maybe? As good a move as any.
Yeah, yeah, yeah.

Part Three

ON OUR WAY HOME

Bowtie (5)

The manhunt for Bowtie has now stretched across six states in the Midwest. There are some unreliable reports of sightings, including one at an Aryan Brotherhood encampment in Idaho and another at a Peoria Chuck E. Cheese. The news coverage is breathless, continuous. Lots of Twitter exultation at the prospect of his demise, along with the predictable cancel culture pushback. His network has issued a reward for information but it's a pretty chintzy take—$10,000—which suggests they maybe don't like him any more than we do. The police are making optimistic noises, *these people usually turn up*, and so on, but bloody bowtie or not, we know the truth, NevskyPete. It's just a matter of time.

Rapprochement

It took a little doing, but I arranged a conference call between my former therapist and my former rabbi. If I was going to leave the underground, I needed a little support and reassurance. I needed witness. The conjoining of the two people who were completely focused on me and my needs, spiritual and mental. My therapist asked a few pointed questions. She kept asking me if I was a danger to myself or others, and I assured her I wasn't, even though I found the question ludicrous. We are *all* a danger *all* the time, with every step we take, every move into the world brings consequences, anticipated, intended, or otherwise. The very act of *being* is fraught with peril. The peril is the point. My rabbit friend nodded and approved of all her questions, affirmed her every word, and I became convinced he was hitting on her. He wanted to know about atonement. Had I reckoned with the error of my ways, was I prepared to make good? I couldn't answer, whatever the hell that meant, because at that moment all I could imagine was the two of them, reverse cowgirl, on the same couch in her office where I'd sat sullenly, unwilling or unable to open up to her. So, the two of them filled my silence with some jocular banter, and they were still going at it when I quit the call.

Now I look around this empty room, which has been empty all along, even with me in it. My meager possessions—a change of clothes, my electronics, and my bankroll—fit into a duffel bag with room to spare. None of it ever made a real dent in the emptiness. I need only sling it over my shoulder, hoist up my Höfner case, and slip out into what's next. I stand there shivering for a final moment in this freezing room, replaying all of it, the lost, enraged hours all merged into a vast gray cloud of nothing, no beginning, middle or end, just this enduring disconnection, one not so easily left behind. I step into the corridor, closing the door behind me.

Apollo sits inside his lobby workstation behind a pane of smudged safety glass. He averts his eyes as I approach, even though I'm fully clothed for once. I slide my key across the counter to him, and I stand there for a moment, taking him in one last time. It's not his fault, this bit part he's been assigned in my drama. Nor is it his fault that he has something to hang his life on, some meaning or purpose or point, however lowly it might be. Is he my better? Maybe. It matters less and less. He is, as my wife used to say, merely a *Person Doing His Best*. He seems to read my thoughts because precisely at this moment, he raises his eyes to meet mine. He takes my key, and I nod at him. A deep and meaningful nod, rich with implication, with acceptance, even. He inhales to speak and ready myself for the acknowledgment I know is coming, our rapprochement.

"Forwarding address?"

Guillotines

It's a three hour bus ride to The Festival. I buy two seats, one for me, one for my Höfner, just like Yo Yo Ma does for his cello. This is what I tell myself, that it's ol' Yo Yo and me all the way, but mostly I just don't want any of my unwashed brethren to sit beside me and try to engage me. There are those who love humankind but hate people; and there are those who love individual people but hate humankind. Me, I hate the whole stinking rotting pile, the macro and the micro. So I press myself into the seat, a small, unapproachable ball not unlike my dying roly poly. I feel a pang for my poor Audi, probably still sitting and decomposing in that Walmart parking lot where I left it at the start of all of this. Yet there's something quite real, palpable, about sitting here on these worn fabric seats, the heady exhaust of carbon monoxide wafting through the bus. And although I know I'm not really one of them, I do feel a strange and tenuous bond to my working class shipmates even as I lament my departed luxury ride. *O hypocrite! My brother!* When I hear the names Musk, Bezos, and Gates, I reach for my guillotine. As the infinite ugly flatness of America scrolls past my window, I think about how my life might have unfurled if only I weren't so awful, so angry. So scared. What would *that* life look like? My phone glows hot in my hand, plugged into the seat charger.

Billy Budapest

A voice, between the cracks, from the seat in front of me.

Hey.

I ignore it. The whisper comes again, louder, more insistent.

Hey.

I will myself not to look at its source, clocked him on the way in. A sallow graybeard. Chest slipped down to his waistband. Thinning perm. Wearing a Shea Stadium T-shirt, old enough to have been there. Disturbing fanboy vibes.

1965 Höfner bass. 500/1, right-handed.

I'm impressed, in spite of myself. How can he possibly tell if it's right or left handed through the case? I catch the pressure of a shrug against the seat in front of me.

I know stuff.

Now I begin to wonder, is he actually speaking to me? Or am I imagining all this? What stuff can a guy like this possibly know?

The usual. Secrets of past and present. The music of the spheres. That kind of thing.

He finally turns in his seat to face me, grins. Going to the festival, he says, more a statement than a question. Me, too. I'm Billy. Billy Budapest. He extends a grubby, nail-bitten hand between the seats. I suppress a shudder and shake it wordlessly. If Billy notices my silence, he doesn't remark on it, doesn't need to, he's off and running on an exuberant monologue about how he's been going to the festivals since they started and boy have they fallen off, the dealer's room a shadow of its former greatness, but when you can buy anything you want online who needs to go to what is basically a glorified swap meet even if the kids have no idea about the thrill of pawing through a box of LPs and landing on a pristine Butcher Cover or some other rarity and the hotels were better back in the day but the crowds are smaller now as the fans are sorta dying off, I guess it'll be my turn soon enough, he adds with a grim chuckle.

He's still talking when we pull into the bus station. Something about him feels familiar though I can't quite place it.

Room (2)

By the time I reach the hotel that hosts The Festival, there's a light dusting of snow on the ground, with a much bigger storm promised within the next twenty-four hours. As I walk along the edge of the building toward the entrance, I look for my ficus, my marker of that terrible day. The hotel has been re-landscaped, all gravel and tiny architectural bushes that look like set dressing from a cheap science fiction movie.

Fans are already milling around the hotel registration desk, waiting for the day's festivities to start up. I can feel their interested eyes on me, on my Höfner case. They are mostly cut from Billy's cloth, fading cheeseburger hippies, bedecked with buttons, T-shirts, gear. Unselfconscious in their adoration. I keep my eyes on the ground as the desk clerk hands me my room key, gives me directions to my room.

The hotel PA has been commandeered, and the albums play round the clock. It's the first time I've heard these songs in who knows how long. The sensory wash makes me dizzy as forgotten harmonies fill my ears. The songs are green with life, sparkling with an effervescence undiminished by time or absence. Like they were recorded yesterday. No. Are being recorded right now, at this moment, everywhere, again and eternally. I hurry through the corridors, and my hands are trembling by the time I reach my room and insert the key card. I leap in and lean against the closed door as though I've been chased here by a mob. Thou shalt not thaw, dammit.

Slowly, I recover myself. The light is strange in this room, not natural sunlight at all, even with the curtains thrown open; it's an antiseptic light, flat and white, that neither warms nor illuminates. I enter with trepidation. I am so used to my cold, tattered squat. There's something almost deafeningly expansive about this room in all its obscene luxury. A proper bed. Carpeting. Temperature controls. A full bathroom, sparkling clean. I spend the first fifteen minutes walking the room end to end. It's a football field, and I don't know where to settle into it. I sit on the edge of the bed, connecting my phone and my laptop to the wireless. The internet connection is terrible. The hellsite refuses to refresh. I am, for the moment, blind, deaf, dumb as fuck. I'm still cold, shivering even with the thermostat cranked up. I notice a stream of ants moving across the writing table.

Howdy neighbor. I feel Billy's voice tickle my brain. He's in the room next door. I don't know how I know this, but I know it. At length, I can hear him masturbating. He's a howler, that Billy. I envy his release.

Lazy Dynamite

Pete doesn't take the stage for another three hours, so there's time to kill. I pause in front of a flyer advertising his band's performance. *The world's foremost soundalikes*, the cheap copy crows. Such a dubious distinction. The best imitation. The best forgery. The best fake. I might not be much, but I'm no fake.

I collect my festival badge and ride the escalator down to the stuffy meeting room level. Here the rooms have unbearably grandiose names: The Horizon Room. The Everest Room. Yet each opens onto a dingy little hovel, conference room chairs and folding tables strewn about. In The Rushmore Room, a self-published author lectures a dozen stragglers about his 786-page book devoted to a stand-in drummer who spent thirteen days on their Australian tour. In another, a panel discussion debating who was the most spiritual of the four, each offering detailed Power Point slides to bolster their case.

In The Yosemite Room, a single microphone is set up, and a line of musicians fills the aisle, awaiting their turns. I know this place: the soundalike contest auditions. Morbid curiosity takes hold, and I slide into the last row, half-sitting on the end chair, ready to leap off it and flee. Instead, I sit there for nearly an hour, watching act after act cycle through, riveted.

The level of talent in the room is, to be generous, uneven. There are a few with that spark of something; and a few for whom the only decent thing to do is avert your eyes and applaud lightly. What they all share, however, is a skin-crawling earnestness. They are so unguarded and so heartfelt it makes me want to stick a spork in my eyes. I think of my earnest wife, my earnest kid (before her rages), even that earnest fraud WillyBee. Was I ever like this? Is it beautiful or embarrassing or hopeless or *#fuckmew-hataloadofnerds*? I want to retreat to *thumbsthumbsthumbs* but No Service thwarts me. A father and daughter perform an acoustic duet of an early single, flat and out of time, and they love each other and the music so much and I know one of us—*one of us*—is a sad, pathetic…

My eyes fall on a trio awaiting their turn. Things have changed. Once the sole province of young white boys, this contest is diverse in gender and in race. The trio, maybe in their early twenties, has a Japanese guitarist, a female bassist and a Black drummer. They whisper to each other, laughing, sharing private jokes, trying to mask their nerves, and I know them, I've been them, I miss them, I miss them so fucking much and they get called to take the stage—*Ladies and Gentlemen, please welcome Lazy Dynamite!* —and they burst into my favorite early period single and they've won before the first ten bars are done and the room is on its feet and the friends are glowing, thrilled smiles and abandon and before I know it, I'm up on my feet hurrying out of the room, the hallway a wet, tear-smeared haze. My kingdom for a ficus.

Gifts

Shaken, I wander into the Dealers Room. When I was here as a teen, the floor was packed. You were lucky if you get close enough to see a table's offerings. Now, fewer than twenty tables are spread through the room. Every single one is presided over by a wan, middle-aged dude slumped in a folding chair, scrolling through his phone as a smattering of randos linger, engage in conversations and anecdotes and stories of this rare pressing and that out of print book. It has the verve of a prison library.

Billy, of course, is here. The little shit is actually wearing a fanny pack. I mean, does he have no loved ones at all? He paws enthusiastically, as advertised, through bins of LPs, absorbed in his hunt. He has a few stashed under his arms. What can be missing from the collection of a guy like that? It's at this moment that he looks up and sees me, smiles, and waves me over. Despite a wave of preemptive weariness, my feet move his direction, and I approach the table, slowing down but not stopping for fear of being engaged in conversation by one of the vendors.

Gifts, Billy explains, gesturing toward his underarm albums. It's always nice to give a gift, right?

I shrug. What does this person want from me?

Actually, he raises a finger as if just remembering, I grabbed this one for you. He hands me a copy of a legit terrible solo album. Perhaps the worst of all of them. I remember the universal scorn that greeted its release.

Thanks for the turd, Billy. You fuckin' complete me.

He leans in close and taps on the album cover portentously. There's a message here, dude. Can't you see it? It's kind of beautiful.

I briefly scrutinize the cover, but I don't want to play. I'm getting tired of Billy's insistent, gnomic good cheer and I start to hand the album back. He shakes his head, won't take it. Instead, he gets in close, a little too intimate for my liking, and whispers with an almost infinite friendliness. He holds the album over his face, speaks from behind it, a grade-school ventriloquist.

I'm the same guy who made all that stuff you love, he says in a dreadful Liverpool accent. He lowers the album and hands it back to me.

Everyone whiffs, he says. Even the great ones. *It's okay.*

He wanders off, whistling. Pete takes the stage in an hour. Ficus, man. I mean *focus*.

GIGO

I'm gloomy and weary by the time I sit down in the hotel restaurant. I don't have much appetite, but I need to get in some dinner before the show and figure out what to say to Pete. It's a generic institutional dining room, the kind you'd see under a government office. I grab the last open table, a small two-top in the rear right by the kitchen door. I sit with my back to the room and peruse the coffee-stained paper menu. My server looks like he belongs on Harley, burly, hairy and pierced, but attends me with solicitous dispatch. He checks in on me frequently and concludes every interaction with a heartfelt "I appreciate you" that makes me want to smack him. I'm wondering about the bush-league hospitality consultant who trained him when Billy drops into the empty seat opposite me.

"Mind if I join you? The place is packed." He looks around with satisfaction, the attendance gratifying to him, as though he's had something to do with it. I look up at him, limp cheeseburger lettuce dangling from my lips and, too taken aback to object, I find myself nodding.

"Awesome, man. Thanks. Hey, Jesse!" he shouts to our server who presently materializes at our table. A storm of effusive high-fives follows. Although Billy arrived the same time I did, it seems these two have known each other forever. Billy's order is taken, and Jesse disappears in a cloud of "I appreciate yous." Billy seems to read my expression because he shakes his head.

No man, it's just like I said: I know stuff.

I slowly raise my eyes to meet Billy's and propose that we pass the meal in silence. He's welcome to the seat but not to my companionship, so how about chowing down on a double helping of shutthefuckup?

Billy raises his hands in an "I read you loud and clear" gesture and begins thumbing through the Festival program. I think I'm in the clear and resume chewing my rubberburger.

Thing is…

I look up at him meaningfully and set my burger down. There is no thing.

Thing is… you seem like a man headed for disappointment is all.

This one surprises me. How do you figure?

Look around this place. You know why people come here, right?

I shrug, feeling stupid. I'm sure my answer isn't the one he's looking for. Developmentally arrested lame-ass fanboys.

They come to relive the past. The happy *past. You get it?*

I'd shake my head, but I won't give him the satisfaction.

This is a place of joy, *man. That's why they come. Not you, though. Been a long time since you felt the joy.*

It's not why I'm here, you little shit. I have unfinished business with a certain pudgy bassist cum killer. I stand to leave. Presumptuous little shithead.

I'm just saying. Garbage in, garbage out.

I turn and march from the dining room, shreds of dignity trailing behind me. I don't turn to acknowledge Jesse as he appreciates me all the way out the door.

First Set

The ballroom is pretty packed for the first of two sets. I wander around the perimeter, leaning on a column here, ducking behind a display there. I'm too anxious to sit, intent on remaining unseen. There's a palpable excitement in the room—the end of day live show is a festival highlight—and I feel the scorn exploding within me. These sad little losers on their pathetic nostalgia trip. I think about the inviting doomscroll heating up my pocket, the infinite timeline of woe, of hatred, of injustice, and I wonder how anyone can possibly care about this facsimile life, this bit of pretend. Still, when the lights go down, a predictable cheer swells and rises as Pete and his four bandmates take the stage and plug in. There's something irritatingly cherubic about Pete, the face of a chubby-cheeked toddler perched atop a fifty-something dad bod in Cuban heels. They count off the first number, and we're underway, the usual chronological revisiting of greatest hits. I'm furious as I watch him, absolutely seething, as I pick out every minuscule de-fect in his performance, real or imagined—off the beat, a tad flat, that rictus grin. But within three of four songs, there comes an unclenching. The fact is that Pete is in his element. The fact is that Pete is pretty fucking good at this. The fact is that songs he sings are programmed so deeply into the *terroir* of my life that it comes as no surprise to find my foot tapping involuntarily. By the halfway point of the set, I catch myself quietly humming through a harmony line. I'm aware of a thousand microscopic cracks in my rigid facade. I find an empty chair on the aisle and again I perch on the very edge of it, as though it's too hot to sit on. And still the fucker plays on, and I'm aware that my trembling fingers are keeping time against my thigh. The aisle is filled with dancers who have formed an impromptu mosh pit at the edge of the stage. One dancer draws my attention. His movements are ungainly, spasmodic, and I wonder if he's some kind of mental defective, and I feel a flash of pity until it occurs to me that perhaps this is simply what unselfconscious joy looks like and then I pity myself for being unable to tell the difference. I strain for a closer look, thinking if I can look into this person's eyes, maybe I can tell what's what. It's Billy, naturally, and he grins this madman's smile as he continues to wave and jerk and shimmy like a palm tree plugged into a light socket. The movement tugs at me, invites me to join. I can't move.

G: *Want Daddy to tell you.*
Me: *Piss. Off.*

I Want to Tell You

Intermission. A twenty minute break between sets. I think about approaching Pete, but I lose my nerve. The setting isn't private enough for our business.

The room has emptied a bit, people stretching their legs, having a smoke. I sit alone in my row on this cheap ballroom chair, stiff-backed, hard bristling felt. I'm vibrating, buzzing, feel a bit dizzy, sick to my stomach, as though the music has loosened something within me, releasing built up toxins into my blood. There's a crumbling within me, a sense of something slowly giving way, unraveling, battlements being knocked over. I reach for my phone, hands shaking, need to shore up the walls but No Service No Service No Service No Service No Service…

Billy has disappeared for the moment, but there's no shortage of doppelgängers in his absence. Fading middle-aged graybeards, festooned in buttons and caps and chatting earnestly about bootleg takes and rare pressings and are these the only choices available to me, earnest fanboy or solo rager? Cheap happiness or lofty suffering? The moment Pete and crew set down their guitars, the PA sprang back to life with its constant stream of music, that music, their music, and hearing it now in this empty room fills me up in an unaccountable fashion; the originals underscoring all of Pete's shortcomings yet heightening my sense of his devotion, his tribute, his what did Billy call it, joy.

For the first time in months or longer, memories uncloud, swirl into form, and I can see things I was sure I'd forgotten. When the kid was just a toddler, maybe three and half years old, we'd play these rounds of *Name That Tune*. I would play their songs for her on my phone and, within a line or two, she'd say the title, and I would applaud and she'd spin with delight. I taught her the whole catalog, American and UK, the obscure ones, the b-sides, the rarities. Every now and then, I'd play one she hadn't yet mastered, and she'd look to me, patiently, for a hint. Finally, she'd say, "Want Daddy to tell you." At that age, she hadn't mastered her pronouns and thought that she was called "you." Denied my No Service Hellsite, I pull up a video of one of our games on my phone instead. I haven't looked at this in years, but now I watch our exchange from so long ago, another child, another father. And then it comes, as I know it will:

Want Daddy to tell you.

This simple request, plaintive and vulnerable. So trusting in my authority, my ability to provide the answers. Well, Daddy has nothing to tell you, not anymore. The only things Daddy knows are terrible, hate-filled, toxic. Other than exit camper strategy, there's nothing useful I can offer you.

Daddy needs a fucking drink. Where's the bar in this joint?

Woolton (2)

The promised blizzard has materialized. Sheets of white are visible through the windows of the most depressing hotel bar in the Northern Hemisphere. On the big screen TVs, CNN continues its breathless Bowtie Coverage. I hear something about a new lead, authorities in pursuit of credible information, but I can't focus, it doesn't connect. The heater is broken, stuck on high, and the sweltering bar is vacant, unbearable. I nevertheless claim a seat at the edge of the bar, order a well scotch from Jessie, who has switched shifts from the dining room. The Johnnie Red tastes like month-old warm piss, burns my throat. I regard my trembling hand clutching the shot glass—is this what detox feels like? The spiritual DTs? Sweat trickles down my forehead, and I think about wandering out into the cold snow, lying down, and vanishing into freezing wet oblivion. Right around there, where my ficus once stood.

I tap on the bar, indicate another round of piss. But before I can pay, a blue satin arm slides a credit card across the bar.
I've got this one.
I turn to face Pete, done up in full Pepper regalia.
Long time.
I nod. He points to his costume.
Still fits. Crazy, right?
That's one word for it. I sip my drink, heart racing. There's so much I want to ask him, so much I need to know. But I'm frozen. Man of action my ass.
You ever hear from the guys? he asks. I shake my head. Not for years. He nods and for a moment, we sip in silence, the first of several uncomfortable pauses. Now that he's here, face to face at last, I can't think of a single thing to say to him. I blink the sweat from my eyes. Eventually, he speaks again.
Did you like the set?

It seems an odd, narcissistic question to ask given the epic business between us, but he has earned his tribute. I turn and face him, looking him directly in the eyes and speak the truth:

"It was great."

He relaxes a bit, relieved and raises his glass.

To Woolton. We drink. Another epic pause.

You know, I was worried about you, those messages you sent sounded a little… but I mean to see you now, well, you look okay. Normal. Are you okay?

I could answer him reflexively, sharp and angry, of course I'm ok and just what have you been getting up to out there, you blood-thirsty, doughy assassin? I look him over, taking his measure, wondering about this web I've spun around him. It's possible, he's a decent size, potentially powerful guy. And Dallas, right? He was there. At length, I shrug and drain my glass. I wonder if Pete notices my shaking hands.

"No. Not okay."

He waves to the bartender for another and leans in close. Here it comes. I think he's going to confess it all and, in a way, I suppose he does, though not the way I'm expecting.

Listen, I want to… He stares into his drink, a bit helpless, a bit sad. It might be moving if he wasn't dressed head to toe in a blue satin marching band costume. He seems unaffected by the stifling heat of the bar.

Look, I'm sorry. I really am.

I turn to him with surprise. Where is he going with this? What wily rook sacrifice has he planned for me? Need to focus, keep up.

What we did to you that day, it was terrible. I've regretted it for years. All my life, really. His voice catches a bit as he speaks. We were kids and stupid and selfish. We thought ripping off the Band-Aid was the way to go, less time to think, less it would hurt. He shakes his head.

I cling to the bar, reeling, swallow the rest of my drink. I don't understand. Of all the things Pete could have done next, a fucking apology? That never occurred to me, not in my wildest dreams. This isn't what I came here for.

Right?

The authorities have a lead.

Pete glances at his watch. He sighs and rises. The second set is about to start. I'm drenched, soaked as though breaking a fever. He places his hand lightly on my shoulder.

Please forgive me.

I think I nod. I must acknowledge him in some fashion because he hurries out of the bar, past Bowtie's pugnacious mug on the TV set, leaving me in this blasted hellscape. I glance up and notice Billy in a corner booth, grinning like a madman, waving at me as he slurps from a fruity umbrella drink. *Would you like to know how this ends?*

Second Set

1

Somehow, I make my way back to the ballroom for the last set. I'm not at all sure how it happens, but at some point the bar falls away and I'm back in my seat as Pete & Co plug in and tune up. Everything in me is thrumming, confused, mildly electrified by our exchange in the bar, his plaintive request: *Please forgive me.* I watch as he breaks into his first number, and I know before he reaches the chorus that I do. It's an impulse, not a thought; a vibration breaking through a brick wall years thick. How can I not? Whatever he may or may not have done, look at him go, all smiles, head bobs and high notes, truly living his best self, saying hello to my goodbyes. I'd sing it along with him if I had just a little more nerve. For now, I settle for a semi-private hum-along. I sink into my seat, unclenching, unspooling. Looking around myself for the first time in years.

2

A few numbers later, they play my favorite of all their songs. An entire verse goes by before I realize I'm holding my breath, thoughts turning to friends and lovers.

I brought them here once, when the kid was maybe seven or so. Why not, I thought? They loved the music, too. They were, I think, a bit bewildered by the hermetic adoration, but they both found things to enjoy. The kid dug the live performances though she knew, even at that age, that the originals were better. My wife, I think, simply enjoyed seeing me enjoy something.

I'd forgotten all of this. I was sure it was gone forever.

And now, though I'm sure I'm imagining it, as Pete sings the closing verse, I feel them here, see them, up there in the mosh pit, holding each other and swaying to this song. Madness, I'm sure, a pure illusion, this conjoining of what's lost and what's now. But it really does look like them. My angry purple-haired kid, dancing with her eyes closed.

I won't approach them. I can't. If I'm wrong, I'll be embarrassed. If it's them, I'm unwelcome. I slide down in my chair as the song comes to its close, I really do love them more.

Ugh. So many feels.

Please forgive me.

Funhouse

They were, in fact, sad to see me go. How can I have forgotten this? I'd planned to skulk out under the cover of night. I knew that if I stayed, I would destroy them, ants and family. So I tiptoed out, stole into the night like a cowardly thief. Leaving behind the terrible mess I'd made.

I stopped into the kid's bedroom. Wednesday morning, five o'clock. She sleeps the sleep of the dad (sorry, autocorrect for dead), and I knew I wouldn't wake her. So I stood before her bed, a cliché watching her sleep, loathing the sentimentality of the gesture but unable to leave without seeing her one last time. I lingered for what felt like ages, studying her sleeping back until I gradually came to realize she was awake, rigid, crying ever so quietly.

I will her to ask me to stay. All I need is a word from her and I can set it all down, try again, try harder but she doesn't say a word and so I turn to leave and I find Liza in the doorway, watching me watching her, this funhouse mirror of cliché, her eyes seeing me as she always does, more clearly than I see myself: A person doing his best. But it's not nearly good enough. Not for them.

Bye bye.

Whispers

Show's over. Back in my room, I can't sleep. I am overloaded, circuits firing wildly. Everything makes a kind of sick, broken sense now, how I became unmoored from my memories, my past, my self, by living in this relentless now. And even as They start to flood back, repopulating my scorched insides, I also feel the virus of hate and fear reaching for my throat, not ready to release me.

My phone. It's still there. It's always been there, never leaves me. I pick it up and fuck this shitty third world internet bullshit. I can barely get down and post what I think, sweaty fingers slipping across the screen…

Gsshrdddng ffff heeeennnb

1:19 AM · Dec 3, 2019

My Höfner case stands propped in the corner. I could swear the bass is rattling around inside, demanding to be let out. It wants to speak to me. Has things to say. *Put me in, coach!* I squeeze my eyes shut, grab my head, don't make me listen, I can't and I won't, you bastard, but now the ants join in, marching in druidic patterns around the case and whispering *sing sing sing* and I won't do it you can't make me and then I'm in the hallway, case under my arm, headed to what, to destiny or disaster.

Burning Raincoats

I hear them before I see them, but I knew they'd be there. The late night open mic singalong, a staple of the festival. Grab your guitar, join the group, play until you crash. It's coming on 2 a.m. and there are dozens of them, milling around, strumming, singing, just listening. An empty conference room with an out of tune piano. What they lack in talent, they make for with energy. A woman who reminds me of my kindergarten teacher picks out an intro on the piano, some guitars join in. There's even a teenager with a sax, lost among the graybeards, blowing for dear life. Billy, of course, is smack in the middle of the action, transported. And the voices, all those voices, a rising chorus, their gusto an infinitely renewable resource.

I sit on the periphery, wanting to join and loathing them. I feel the eyes on my bass case, the curiosity. What's he got in there? But I can't quite bring myself, even as I run through each bass line in my head as I listen, every note just where I left it. My hand trembles again, but now it's not #detox, it's desire, something pure. How many years has it been? I unhook one clasp of the case, then a second. I can't do better than that, not yet. A murmur passes through the crowd. I turn in the direction of the commotion and there's Pete and his pals, dressed in civvies, come to check out the jam session. And why not? This was once their province, all those years ago. They drop into chairs and with a "don't mind us, proceed" wave, the music continues. Pete looks my way, makes eyes at my case, and with a friendly head bob, urges me to the mic. I shake my head. But Pete persists. He whispers something to one of the guitar players who delightedly hands over his acoustic six-string. Pete takes his natural place behind the mic and explains we have a special guest here tonight, the bass player from his very first band, and please welcome him to the mic for an important piece of unfinished business. Every eye in the room swivels my way, and my impulse is to bolt, but I hear myself opening the remaining clasps and hoisting my Höfner from its case. Lying on the felt is my daughter's torn drawing from all those years ago, yellowed tape jigsawing it in place: *Why so sad?*

Someone hands me a patch cord, and I plug in as Pete begins to play. Smart move, don't give me too much time to think. It's an acoustic duet from their late period, nominally a love song but has always felt more to me like a tribute to friendship. The original has no bass guitar on it, but I improvise an accompanying line and Pete smiles approvingly. I love the feel of the bass in my hands again; the perfect proportion of the narrow neck; the fat, sweet, full sound of those wonderful flat wound strings. We settle into the vocal, sharing the mic. Pete takes the high harmony, I take the low and try not to cry.

I step back to allow Pete to take the middle eight, I know he'll do it right, and yet it astonishes me how good he still sounds, the sweetness of his voice. It sounds like he's singing it for me, I'm sure he is. Just this once it's not my ego. We really do have memories, Pete and me. And I see that he cannot be Nevsky because he is truly happy, and the truly happy don't do these kinds of mad, bad things. My eyes return to the kiddo's torn up drawing in my Höfner case, and I foolishly scan the crowd for Them, and though I know I won't find them, I don't stop hoping because to stop hoping will be to slip back into all that what was, and I've had enough.

Why so sad?
I have never stopped missing them. But you knew that already.

Pete and I steer into the last verse, and now I can't help it, I'm crying, I can feel the final release inside me. All the other guitars in the room have joined in, and the unified strumming urges us on, says together says forward says tomorrow says love and we are so carried away that we fuck up the lyrics, which were always hard to remember. Pete sings "wearing raincoats" and I sing "burning matches" and the audience hears us "burning raincoats"

and now we are all laughing hard, losing the thread, wiping different tears away as we whistle the closing through giggles. Out of
the corner of my eye, I think I can see Billy nod at me
and walk away.

Punchline

Did you really think I was gonna go all Mark David Chapman on his ass? What the fuck is wrong with you people?
(It's catching, though, isn't it?)

Surrender

I'm heading back to my room via a glassed in skybridge that connects the hotel rooms to the function rooms when I am awash in lights and sirens. Below me, four police cars skid into the hotel courtyard, red and blue lights flashing, and I think back to the news report in the bar, new leads, credible information, and of course they've come for me, no other way to read this, and I'm ready to be done with all this, *atonement*, isn't that what my rabbi said, time to face up and make good and all that nonsense and so I prepare myself to confess and surrender peacefully when I notice that the officers have guns drawn and are chasing Billy through the parking lot. He holds his hands high up in the air to show he's no threat but he's running ungainly figure eights in the snow and laughs as he waves maniacally to me as I look down on this Keystone Cops circle jerk. At length, one of the cops produces a taser, and Billy goes down like a roped calf, twitching in the snow. They hoist him up roughly, cuff him, and as they guide him to the back of a cruiser, he shrugs at me with a wink and an "I've got ya" look of a man taking one for the team. The cars speed away, and all is quiet once again in the forecourt, snow dusting the tracks as though it never happened. I should be mad at the little shit for stealing my thunder but truth is I'm going to miss that crazy bastard.

By the time I return to my room, the ants are swarming everywhere. I strip down and lie naked on the bed and I surrender myself to them, let them crawl all over me. It tickles and before long, I laugh. Finally, I feel warm.

Bowtie Coda

I turn on the TV and check CNN. It's over. They've found Bow-tie. Convinced of a global Jewish conspiracy, he went off the grid with his mountainous cache of kiddie porn. He was found in a Charlottesville motel room, hanging naked from the bathroom door. Auto-erotic asphyxiation but, miraculously, not dead. The paramedics arrived in time, revived him (but not before one of them tweeted a photo of him *en flagrante*, a pale, naked piñata gone viral). The police arrested him on child pornography charges and a right-wing energy drink magnate has already set up a legal defense fund. His network has put him on "hiatus." Not dead in a dumpster, but I'll take it.

Is it possible, though, that there's the tiniest spark of pity now flaring within me for this confused and broken—

Pffffft. Can't even keep a straight face with that shit. You saw right through it, didn't you? Epiphanies is one thing but c'mon…

Spawn

I'm drifting into a contented sleep when my neglected phone surprises me with a ping, a clarion call breaking through No Service.
Trumpets of angels and all that. Imagine my surprise.

Direct messages > with @mydadissuchanasshole   ✕

You sounded good tonight. I like you singing much
better than I like you tweeting. #Deleteyouraccount
Love, me PS You suck at tech, I've known all along.
And the exit campers will always respawn unless
you tear their hearts out.

Re-Spawn

She was born small and couldn't latch, so she spent the first two nights of her life in the NICU. My wife and I switched off feeding her from a bottle every few hours. My first shift came at 3 a.m. I rested her in my lap and held the bottle for her and perhaps it was the hour and the lack of sleep and the nerves but I had a literal, physical sensation of all of the world being pulled away, like a stage set being struck, so that all that remained was the two of us in the inky void and I was so sure that I had finally found my purpose and that I would move heaven and earth to fill her life with joy, and somehow I fucked it up and lost the thread but my heart hasn't been torn out, not yet, not fully anyway, so maybe I might still re-spawn for her.

Crumbs

While I wait for my room service breakfast, I punch in @NevskySoldier into a bot tracking site I've been avoiding. The result does not surprise me.

Perhaps I've known all along, too. I feel that cascading relief that comes when the unwanted house guest finally gets out of Dodge. A mess left behind to be sure, crumbs on the counter, food in the recycling bin, stains on your towels, everything rearranged just a bit off where it's meant to be. But you can, in fact, clean it up, set everything back the way you like it. It's a hassle, takes some time, but at last the fucker is gone.

Hero

Would you like to know how this ends? I think it's time, and I've got a late checkout. After all, looking back at all of this, all these years, it's all quite *unpleasant*, isn't it? It was probably a mistake to set all this down in this way, though if it's any consolation, writing it down hasn't felt much better than reading it. I certainly wouldn't call it *literary*… more of a wankerama. I suppose the *woe-is-me*-ness of it all is bound to grate after a while. After all, just like that Jesus freak Fyodor said, a novel needs a hero, whereas this laundry list of my failings doesn't make me especially *relatable*, even though this random shitpile that has been my life is *real*, and we don't know what to do with real anymore, do we? On that score, I side with FD, we are all lame-ass invalids, every one of us. We can't bear to be reminded of real life, our families, our work, our jobs, we'd rather be lost amid hashtags and virals and trending. We may talk a good game about "what matters" and "the good fight," but you give us too much reality and we go running back to the safety of *thumbsthumbsthumbs*. I already anticipate your indignation, your rising cries of "Nuh-uh" and "Speak for yourself, biatch" and "Stay in your lane," but c'mon tweeps, I'm not talking about "us" or "y'all" I'm talking about *me*, about having taken this thing as far as it can go, having lived the hellscape with a totality you haven't dared, confusing your cowardice and somnolence for good sense. But maybe, just maybe, I'm the one who's got it right, perhaps only I have come to see that staring into the abyss does nothing more than confirm that the abyss exists, for all the good that will do, like that's some big fucking shock. Whereas left to yourselves, without the Bluebird of Shittiness to guide you and tell you what to think, you'll immediately get lost and confused, won't know what to join, what to hold on to, what to love and what to hate, what to respect and what to despise. So you spend your whole lives trying to fill that broken void inside you with the thing that made the void to begin with— *is designed expressly to create that insatiable hunger*—and I will watch as you waste away into nothingness like I almost did. So how, then, to respond, how to live? Best guess is this is what Yeats was trying to tell me: Be secret and *exult*. Everything matters. Everything is trivial. Everything is joy. Everyone whiffs. Whatever you do, just don't lose the capacity for joy, for wonder. I imagine that's what Liza was trying to tell me in the Zen garden. I think of all the time spent shouting, raging, fulminating, tweeting, when I might have been listening instead. Perhaps that's what Pete meant, what WillyBee meant, what my rabbit meant. What my daughter means. #Deleteyouraccount.

So how *does* this end? I couldn't tell you. Mostly, it really does continue on and on and on, so I might as well stop now. Though maybe, god help me… Is it possible that they were right, that love really is all you need? Simple as that? Right there under my nose the whole time? These thoughts consume me as I shepherd the last of the ants from my room on a bit of card stock, out into the morning sun as the wet snow melts and runs away.

Profile
UGMan
@ugman
This account doesn't exist
Try searching for another.

ACKNOWLEDGEMENTS

Thanks to Jennifer Carson, Amitava Kumar, Simon Lipskar, Marie Mutsuki Mockett, Marisa Silver, Jill Bialosky, Jerry Wheeler, and Christopher Stoddard.

And, for generous support, gratitude to Guild Hall of East Hampton, the City of Santa Monica Department of Cultural Affairs, and Dorland Mountain Arts Colony.

ABOUT THE AUTHOR

Photo by Yanina Gotsulsky

MARK SARVAS is the award-winning author of *Memento Park*, which garnered multiple accolades, including a 2019 American Book Award, and was shortlisted for several other prestigious awards. His debut novel *Harry, Revised* was published internationally to critical acclaim, drawing comparisons to Updike and Roth. A prolific literary critic whose work has appeared in the *New York Times Book Review*, the *Threepenny Review*, and numerous other publications, Sarvas began his career hosting the acclaimed literary blog "The Elegant Variation." He's a member of multiple literary organizations, has judged several notable literary prizes, and currently teaches advanced novel writing at UCLA Extension while holding an MFA from Bennington College. He lives on the Monterey Peninsula.

BOOKS BY ITNA

Urban Gothic: The Complete Stories
Bruce Benderson

Settlers Landing
Travis Jeppesen

The Beads
David McConnell

The Virtuous Ones
Christopher Stoddard

After David
Catherine Texier